FURY AT PAINTED ROCK

Owen Frank had wanted no part of the war at Painted Rock. Neither did he want the silver star on his chest or the role of lawman in this untamed land, but he had been drawn into it. He did wear the badge. And now it was either kill Miles Rankin or be killed himself!

FURY AT PAINTED ROCK

Will Cook

GUNSMOKE

First published by Robert Hale, Ltd

This hardback edition 2004
by BBC Audiobooks Ltd
by arrangement with
Golden West Literary Agency

ISBN 0 7540 8283 0

British Library Cataloguing in Publication Data available.

Printed and bound in Great Britain by
Antony Rowe Ltd., Chippenham, Wiltshire

CHAPTER 1

He entered the town of Painted Rock at sundown, stabled his horse at Longmire's, then walked a half block south to the hotel. There he paused on the broad gallery to look back at the fifty-seven miles of burning desert he had just crossed.

Shouldering his bedroll and saddlebags, he entered the lobby, now flooded with glaring light as the last rays of the evening sun blared through the front windows, deepening the maroon rug, bouncing from the varnished, paneled walls.

He stopped at the desk and palmed a small handbell. A woman's heels rapped on the hard floor in the rear of the building, then a separating door opened and closed. Pausing behind the counter the young woman surveyed him quickly, read him for what it was worth, and spun the register around. In a broad, angular hand, he wrote, Owen Frank, San Angelo, Texas, before laying a gold piece on the blotter.

"You're a long way from home," the girl said.

Frank's eyes came up, hard and clear and somehow suspicious, but in the woman's expression he could read nothing but friendliness.

"By the week," he said, and his voice sounded deep and somewhat rusty, as though he hadn't used it for some time. The sound of it was a surprise even to himself.

"We don't serve meals any more," the girl said. "Not since my father took sick. There's a restaurant two doors down on this side of the street." She was tall, coming nearly to his eyes, and her hair was a pale gold, dangling in braids down her back. Her face was thin and her cheekbones prominent. For beauty, her lips would have had to be fuller, her

5

chin less blunt, the large eyes not quite so widely spaced. But it was a pleasant face; despite the lack of symmetry there was quality, and a deep capacity for life that he sensed rather than saw.

"That will be fine," he murmured, and took the key she handed him. Shouldering his plunder he turned, meaning to ascend the stair, but her voice reached out and held him, bringing him about to face her.

"Mr. Frank—did you cross the desert?"

"Why, yes, I did," he said, and a frown made deep tracks across his forehead. "Does it matter which way a man comes to town?"

"Around here it does," she said quietly. "Forget it."

Turning again toward the stair, he felt her eyes on him and didn't care. On his face, burned to a walnut hue by years in the sun, there was that studied gravity that comes to a man when he has had too much trouble and never enough money. Beneath his roll-brimmed hat were eyes a startling shade of blue with splinters of light in them. His nose was straight and without a break and beneath it a full mustache flowed past the corners of his lips, tawny like his hair.

He moved deeper into the hall, his Mexican spurs ringing against the bare floor, and beneath this sound the creak of his gun harness was faint, the muffled protest of dried leather.

Inserting his key, Owen Frank turned the lock, toeing the door open and closed before depositing his blanket roll and saddlebags on a straight backed chair. Glancing around the room, he saw with that one sweep of his eyes the hand-planed boards, the pine dresser with its cracked marble top, and the brass bedstead in the far corner. A wash-faded towel hung limply by the commode. The wall by the head of the bed, as well as the window sill, was covered with jackknife artistry, made by men like himself, lonely and a little afraid, and just passing through to another place equally as lonely.

He removed his coat, rolled his shirt sleeves, took off his string tie and poured water from the pitcher into a porcelain bowl. After washing, he dried himself on the towel, then painstakingly brushed away all signs of travel from his clothes. He wore a dark suit with a white shirt and black tie. His clothes were old but in good repair. His flat-crowned

6

hat lay on the dresser, the brim sagging a little past the edge.

Around his waist a shell belt drooped slightly, the once full loops showing vacancies, like a small boy who had lost his front teeth. On his right hip there rested a gun in a carved, Mexican holster. Removing this, Owen Frank rocked open the loading gate, rotated the cylinder in a series of dry clicks and spilled the blunt-nosed cartridges onto the marble topped commode. After pulling the cylinder pin, he took a cleaning rod and rag from his saddlebag and spent a careful fifteen minutes erasing all sign of the desert dust.

Darkness crept into the room while he assembled the gun. He lighted the lamp and crossed to the window to look down at this town. He had been in a dozen like it in the past year, pausing for a time, then going on. On to where? He worried a little about it, for this urge to move on was like a hand at his back.

Splitting the town was a narrow ribbon of loose dust, now a dull gray in the last fading light. Flanked on each side, blunt-faced buildings sat shoulder to shoulder, rising darkly against the sky. To the west, the desert spread its flatness, now barren and lifeless as night lowered its purple mantle. To the east, giant bastions of rock rose to heights that seemed staggering, and past them the land dipped and rolled, lowering into green valleys.

On the street, a group of ponies stood before the saloon, three-footed and half asleep. There was some traffic on the street, and to the north a splatter of lights showed another camp away from town. In the stillness of early evening he could hear the muted sound of voices coming from the camp, a mingling of laughter and the movement of men.

Tied before the hardware store was a high-sided lumber wagon with a roll of wire fencing in the back. From beneath the overhang of the hardware store a man emerged, in bib overalls, wearing a square-cut beard. He rolled another bundle of fencing to the tailgate and with a mighty surge of muscle hoisted it to the bed and closed the back of the wagon.

The doors of the saloon flapped idly as a heavy man came out, followed by two more. Light filtering through the slats of the door glinted on the pearl-handled guns worn by the heavy man. Glancing down the street where the farmer loaded his fence, the man left the saloon, cutting diagonally across the street. He approached the farmer on an angle, and when he drew near, he jabbed the man suddenly in the small of the back with his elbow.

The blow drove the bearded man against the wagon and the man with the guns walked on, disappearing from Owen Frank's view. A group of cattlemen gathered on the saloon porch, their laughter rippling along the street. The farmer limped to his wagon, mounted with some difficulty and drove out of town.

The rules never change, Frank thought. *A man can ride a thousand miles and find the same pattern everywhere.* He shrugged into his coat and went out, taking the stairs with a loose-muscled roll. The girl stood by the window and she turned to him, giving him a sharp appraisal. He didn't mind the quiet display of reserve, but her suspicion was like a sudden shout.

On impulse he stopped at the desk, both hands gripping the edge. "What's your name?"

"Joanne Avery. Why?"

"That man loading wire," Frank said. "And that other one who came across from the saloon. Who are they?"

He watched her face carefully and saw a door close in her mind, shutting him out. In her eyes there was resentment and pride and a stubborn will that told him she would bend to no man, but around her lips he saw a contradiction.

"The farmer was Fred Meechum," Joanne Avery said. "Sweikert was the man who bumped him."

"Across the desert," Frank said, "people told me there was a war here in the making. Is that right?"

For a moment she studied him. "There's land here and men are willing to kill to keep it. Would you kill to get it?"

A brittleness came into his eyes. "Once, men killed to take mine. Does it matter?"

"You came across the desert," Joanne said without friendliness. "That's the way Sweikert and all of Alvertone's Teepee bunch came. The farmers came from the south and the east. There's a difference."

"Not to me," he said, and walked to the front door. Once on the gallery, he hesitated to give the street a more detailed inspection. To his left and south, the largest building, an old store, reared up on the corner of Riot and Buffalo

8

Streets. Flanking it to the north was a small saddle shop, log, like the rest of these buildings, for in this portion of Idaho timber was plentiful. The feed store sat on the far corner with another hardware store cuddled against it. Farther down, an abandoned livery stable rose in black shadows and behind it were the express freight shed and a corral, almost hidden from view.

Along the east side where he stood, there was the mercantile, a sprawling building with three entrances, the Wells Fargo office, and a small restaurant wedged between it and the sheriff's office on the corner.

On the porch of the saloon across the street, the group of cowmen talked and laughed in loud voices. Owen Frank placed a deliberate attention on them, listening to their jumbled talk and feeling the tension run through the town.

He knew the story well, for it had happened to him. In the beginning the land had been free and a man took what he wanted. But times changed and new people kept coming until a man had to fight or give up. IIe had fought, together with the other cattlemen, but there was no real victory. Pushing one bunch of farmers off the land didn't stop others from following, and then a man had it to do all over again.

At first he had cursed himself frequently for walking away without a backward glance, but now he had convinced himself that he had done the right thing, and if he felt any regret for his decision he hid it well.

Vacating the gallery, Owen Frank angled across the street to the saloon, now bright with squares of lamplight blooming from the windows. The cattlemen stopped talking when he drew near. He placed a deliberate glance on each of them, especially Sweikert. Near Sweikert stood a younger man, barely twenty. On his face was a boldness that Frank couldn't miss. The young man wore a gun tied against his right thigh and he smiled faintly at Frank before the tall Texan nudged the batwings aside and went into the saloon.

Bellying against the bar, Frank smiled. He could read the signs as clearly as newsprint. Sweikert and the young man were not riders, for there was no stamp of hard work in their dress or manner. Frank glanced around the room, noticing the sparse trade, and formed an opinion in his own mind. A dozen men clustered around tables against the wall, some drinking, others pretending to play cards.

Watching them in the mirror, Owen Frank saw that they

9

all looked him over carefully, not an unusual thing, although men were rarely so pointed about it.

The bartender sidled up and Owen Frank said, "The good whisky."

"All my whisky is good," the man said. He was heavy and very fat and his hair was parted severely down the middle, well-oiled and slightly curling where it lay against his forehead.

"Your best then," he amended, and leaned against the cherrywood, a sudden weariness in his back and legs. The bartender poured gingerly and Owen Frank laid a quarter on the bar. Tossing off the drink, he cupped the empty glass in his big hands while the sudden warmth shot through him.

Through the back bar mirror, Frank studied again the men at the tables. A few did not pull their eyes away from him quickly enough and he smiled faintly at this. They seemed to be placing him in their minds, as a man remembers where he sets a chair or a half empty bottle.

Glancing at his own reflection, he saw a man in a dark suit and mule-ear boots, thirty-some—no different from any other man, yet very different.

For in Owen Frank's face there was a knowledge of men that set him apart and made him ride alone. Somewhere along the trail of Owen Frank's thirty years, the lure of easy money had endowed him with sufficient perception to understand a thief. The man who lied was no enigma to Frank, for he could recall times in his own life when he had felt a deep reluctance to face the truth about himself. A man who could kill no longer baffled him, for he had lived long enough to understand the nature of violence.

He, too, appeared to live on the thin edge of violence, and men noted this. Owen Frank attached importance to the little things, the darted glance, the soft murmur of a voice.

Suspecting that the bartender had an eye on him also, Frank signaled him with the barest movement of his finger. "Business is a little dead tonight," he murmured. "This a cattlemen's saloon?"

"The cattlemen use it," the man said. "Maybe it'll brighten up. They're waiting for the stage." He inclined his head slightly toward the front of the building and the Teepee hands outside. "You waiting for the stage too?"

"I'm not going any place," Owen Frank said.

"I didn't think you were," the bartender said, and glanced at the wall clock. "Ten minutes." He whipped his head around as the batwings winnowed. The young man with the tied-down gun came in. Behind him walked a husky man with an arrogant face. Studying him, Frank guessed that he was Teepee and the boss. The bartender moved away. The young man took a position on Owen's left, the other man, farther down.

"Give me a whisky, Felix," he said, and stood with his hands flat along the edge of the bar until it was poured. "Don't stand so close to me, Rankin," the young man said, and the Teepee boss shifted his weight, a clear displeasure on his face. When the bartender moved away again, the young man glanced at Owen Frank, but didn't touch his drink.

"The register at the hotel says you're from Texas. So am I."

"Your two-gun friend from Texas too?"

"Sweikert?" The young man laughed. He had even teeth and his hair was wheat-colored, worn long against his collar. His eyes were bright with humor and a certain devilment, a legacy of all Texans.

"He's rough on farmers," Frank said softly.

"This is cattle country," the Teepee boss said flatly. "I'm Miles Rankin, Alvertone's foreman. You must be the man he sent for." He inclined his head to the young man. "This is Reilly."

Reilly flipped his head around as the batwings banged open once more. A man pulled to a halt just inside. He was a short man, neatly dressed, but somehow his suit didn't quite fit and he acted self-conscious in it. When Owen Frank glanced at the man's shoes he understood why, for they were hob-nailed with brass caps across the toes. A farmer dressed for town.

Setting his drink aside, Reilly moved away from the bar with Rankin, and Frank continued to watch the man in the doorway. The fellow glanced around nervously and then walked to the far end of the bar, rapping for service.

Fastening his eyes on Owen Frank who stood alone now, the man became belligerent. His bulldog jaw took on a stubborn set, and when he puffed out his cheeks the ends of his thick mustache bristled.

"Are you waitin' for me?" the man asked.

"Just drinking," Owen murmured.

Without taking his eyes off Frank, the man said, "Give me a straight whisky, Felix." Spreading his fingers, he groped for the glass and tossed it off.

"What are you staring at?" Owen Frank asked. "Am I supposed to know you?"

Setting his canvas traveling bag on the bar, the man hunched his shoulders as though readying for a fight. "I'm Harry Showers, mister. What the hell are you going to do about it?"

"Nothing," Frank said. "Buy you a drink, maybe."

Showers tipped his head back and laughed. He sobered immediately. "I'll buy my own. Cattlemen's money has a stink to it." Tipping the bottle, he poured a double shot and tossed it off, then started to pour a third.

"Easy, Harry," Felix murmured, taking his wrist. "One's for the chills. Two's for 'what the hell.' But after two a man can't shoot too straight."

"I'll shoot straight at anything that gets in my way," Showers said in a loud voice. Frank leaned on one elbow, sweeping Harry Showers with a sharp glance.

Down the street the rattle of the approaching stage was clear in the sudden quiet. Running a darting tongue over his lips, Showers said to Owen Frank, "I'm gettin' on that stage. Don't try to stop me."

"I'm not going to stop you," Frank said, and frowned when Showers reached up and unbuttoned his coat. The pounding drum of the span drew near; the rattle of chains and bitts was distinct now.

Showers leveled a finger at Owen Frank and shouted, "Take this warning to Burk Alvertone—fool with me and there'll be dead men!"

"Be careful with yourself now," Frank said, and wondered if the man was crazy. He felt the cool wind of danger blow against him, but there was no power in him to halt this.

Across the street, brake blocks squealed and the coach teetered to a rocking halt before the Wells Fargo office. The conversation between driver and agent was low toned but discernible. Other talk could be heard in the street and then a man's yell rose high. "Teepee! Here, Teepee!"

Several of the men at the tables scraped back their chairs

but Miles Rankin's voice was as cool as a winter wind. "Easy, now. There's enough out there to handle those sodbusters."

The men settled back at their tables. Owen Frank watched Harry Showers. Snatching up his canvas satchel, Harry Showers wheeled toward the door. Then he spun around.

"Take this back to Alvertone!" he shouted.

He whipped a gun from a shoulder holster.

Showers' bullet peeled wood from the bar by Owen Frank's elbow and the room bulged with the sudden detonation. Then Showers was in a plunging run and Frank's shot splintered the wildly whipping batwings, going home, for Showers let out a deep grunt and cascaded off the porch.

Making the door in two jumps, Owen Frank ducked out and to one side as Showers fired again, this time from a propped-up position by the hitchrail. The man was down and badly hurt, but determination gave him strength to lift his gun.

Without hesitation, Owen Frank wiped his palm across the hammer twice and Showers was driven back in the dust, his tardy shot whining off the eave of a building before power left him and he lay back, unmoving.

Along the street doors banged open and a crowd began to gather on the run. The saloon emptied in a minute, each man running to what seemed a predetermined position. The farmers were grouped across the street in a cluster of fifty or more. Standing before them were Sweikert and five other men and their presence was enough to keep the farmers in line.

When Reilly and Miles Rankin crossed the street, Sweikert detached himself from the gathering of Teepee riders and approached the saloon, the outflung shop lights reflecting from the pearl-handled guns he wore. Pausing to stare down at Harry Showers, Sweikert fanned his mustache away from his lip with the web between thumb and forefinger.

When he glanced up at Owen Frank, the man's eyes held a veiled pleasure as though he were enjoying a secret joke. "You're worth the money," he said, and grinned lopsidedly before turning to drive through the gathering pack.

From the outer edge of the circle, another man elbowed his way through to look first at Showers, then at Owen Frank. He was a young man in his early thirties, tall and well set up, with a handsome face. He said, "You did a complete job. Alvertone can certainly pick 'em, I'll say that." From the folds of his stylish coat a star peeked out.

"He just pulled a gun and shot at me," Frank said. "I never saw him before in my life."

"I'd like to pin murder on you for this," the lawman said. "But I know Alvertone too well to hope for that." He hunched his shoulders as if he felt cold. "I'm Will Savage, mister. Ask Rankin or any of the Teepee crew about me. This isn't the end of this, believe it or not."

The crowd was silent, listening, and from the far end of the street a horseman paced slowly toward them. Raising his head, Owen Frank watched him approach and knew instinctively that this was Alvertone, for the man edged his horse against the crowd, forcing them to make way for him.

He was an old man, rifle straight in the saddle, and his hair and mustache were white. He looked down at Harry Showers with a detached, disdainful expression. Glancing over at Sweikert, he nodded and the man moved off the saloon porch.

"You've done a good night's work, Burk," Will Savage said, a driving temper in his eyes.

"Someone has," Alvertone murmured, and glanced at Owen Frank. He read the signs in an instant and unerringly singled out Frank as the man who had done the shooting.

"Get your men off the street before there's more trouble," Savage said.

Alvertone smiled and slipped a cigar in his mouth. The flare of the match outlined features that were lean and predatory. His eyes were a flat and chilly gray. "I'll do that when it pleases me," Alvertone said. "Be careful now, Will. I don't like to be pushed at all."

"Get these men off the street," Savage repeated, and waited, his stubbornness making him solid and threatening.

Alvertone puffed his cigar as though considering it. Finally he shrugged. "Why not, Will. Two weeks from now I'll have my own sheriff. I can wait that long."

He made a circular motion with his hand and Sweikert called to the other Teepee men along the street. His heavy voice pushed at the crowd, driving them back. Across the street, the driver of the stage could wait no longer and he yelled to the span, rattling out of town, the sidelights two bobbing cells of brightness to hold back the night.

Mounting, Sweikert led the crew out of town and Owen Frank remained in the street by Harry Showers. Alvertone had not left. He had dismounted and crossed the street to the restaurant.

The farmers still huddled together, waiting, he was sure, for him to move on so they could carry Harry Showers away. Thumbing out the spent loads in his Remington, Owen Frank refilled the cylinder as Fred Meechum left the crowd and came over. Frank stood there, a tall man with a patient face and eyes that were somehow sad.

On Meechum's face there was anger, but beneath that, there was the hopelessness that men feel when all odds are against them and they are powerless to do anything about it. He spoke softly to Frank, a strange thing from a man so large. "Harry was a nice fella, gunfighter."

"I had to do it," Frank said. "He shot first."

"Sure," Meechum said. "I guess I know how things are around here."

"I'm sorry," Frank said, and reholstered his gun while crossing the street.

The crowd of farmers let him through and he went into the restaurant, taking a table against the back wall. Frank placed his hat on an empty chair and went slack bodied, leaning on the oilcloth covered table. The smell of food reminded him of his hunger and he ordered, waiting patiently while it was being cooked. He sat hunched over, massaging his hands with a nervousness he didn't bother to conceal. The afterwash of the fight rolled over him, drawing his nerves out like thin wire, then letting go with the suddenness of an electric shock.

The pattern of men's pride was an old picture to Owen Frank; he possessed a good deal of it himself. A man could ride for a year to forget that he had used a gun, but he could never really ride far enough, for what he is and has been he carries with him wherever he goes.

Showers' pride had pushed him into rashness and he died. Alvertone had the same hard pride, sitting there on his horse with hate flowing like a river around him and not fearing it in the least.

When Frank's meal came, he found that he had no stomach for it. He nursed his coffee, drawing a feeble comfort from it. Behind him, two men rose, their chairs scraping loudly on the floor; then they came alongside Owen

Frank's table. "Wait for me in the saloon, Rankin," Alvertone murmured, and the Teepee foreman went out.

On Alvertone's face there was an unreadable smoothness; only a mild interest bloomed in his eyes. Touching the back of a vacant chair, he asked, "May I?" When Frank nodded, he sat down, shifting the Texan's hat to one side to make room for his arms.

"That was unpleasant out there," Alvertone said, and lit a fresh cigar. "But you'd know all about that, wouldn't you?"

"Would I?"

"You've smelled smoke before," Alvertone said softly. "Somewhere else perhaps, but the place doesn't matter. Once a man gets the smell of blood on him, people can tell it right away."

"Showers leading the farmers?"

Alvertone shook his head. "Meechum leads them." He sighed and signaled the waitress to bring him a cup of coffee. "You can see why I can't give an inch. If a few of them are allowed to settle here, I'll have them swarming over me like locusts. You're a cattleman. You know how it is."

"Sure," Frank said, and moved his cup around in aimless circles. "Down in San Angelo I had nine thousand acres and they started moving in. Fencing the water holes and damming the creeks. I fought 'em. I killed and burned and won, and when I got through I got sick to my stomach at what I'd done." He raised his eyes to Alvertone's and there was no friendliness there for the older man. "I'm not for you, Alvertone. I hope Meechum and Will Savage lick the pants off you."

"So now you ride over hills admiring your shadow on the ground." Burk Alvertone laughed and took his coffee from the girl. "Listen to me, Frank. I don't like this, but I'm doing it. When I came to this country I had to chase the buffalo off to get room to build my house. I didn't walk off no boundary lines. I just waved my hands at the hills and said 'I'll take as far as I can see.' You think this has been my only fight? There were others who wanted what I had and I fought 'em, just like I'll fight Meechum and any sodbuster with a plow tied to his wagon."

"I heard you out on the street," Frank said. "There going to be a turnover in the law pretty soon?"

"Savage is no good," Alvertone said. "No good for me.

You saw the next sheriff—Sweikert." He sipped his coffee, peering over the rim at Frank. "Get that look off your face. That's the only way and you know it is."

"Maybe," Frank murmured. "But a man doesn't have to like it, does he?"

"You're a cool one," Alvertone said, standing up. "Be smart now. I can use you."

"I'm just passing through," Frank said flatly. "Tomorrow I'll be twenty miles from here and this town will be behind me, forgotten."

"You're not like that," Alvertone said. "You won't forget. You'll remember, and wonder what happened." A pale smile lifted his lips. "I'll be over to the saloon until ten, in case you change your mind."

He turned then and went across the street. Owen Frank stared after him until the old man went into the saloon, and then finished his coffee. Placing a half dollar on the table, he took his hat and walked out, going immediately to the hotel.

In the lobby a dozen people were congregated, some townsmen, but the bulk of them farmers. A drab woman sat in a deep, leather covered chair, a half grown boy beside her. When Owen Frank saw her red-rimmed eyes he knew that this was Harry Showers' widow. The ripple of talk faded quickly as he stepped into the room and the faces that swung to him were hard and unfriendly.

Moving from behind the counter, Joanne Avery stepped in front of him, blocking his path. She said, "I wondered what you were when you came to Painted Rock. Now I know. We all know, don't we?"

There was nothing he could say, for he had killed a man. Owen Frank showed no expression, save the sadness in his eyes, and she failed to notice that.

A wild temper gripped her and she battled it. "You were the gunman Alvertone expected, weren't you?"

"No," Owen Frank said. "Harry Showers made a mistake."

"And now he's dead." She clenched her fist. "You're lying. You were sitting at the same table with Burk Alvertone a few minutes ago."

Owen Frank's shoulders rose and fell slightly. "All right, have it your own way. I'm lying, then. That's what you want to believe, isn't it?"

When he moved to step around her, she seized him by the sleeve and hit him in the mouth with her fist. The force of it rocked his head back, but his stony expression did not change. From the corner of his lip a drop of blood seeped past and dripped down his chin onto the maroon rug.

"Do you feel better now?" he asked in his soft voice. "I hope you do because it can't change the way I feel about it."

She did nothing to stop him when he turned and mounted the stairs. Opening his door with the key, he stepped inside and locked it, realizing too late that he had made a serious mistake.

The room was filled with the strong odor of stale cigar smoke—and he did not smoke cigars.

CHAPTER 2

When the first scent of cigar smoke registered, Owen Frank tried to whirl, but someone leaped astride him, bearing him to the floor while locking him in a grip that threatened to break his ribs. Another man shuffled around the room while the first held him, squirming but helpless. There was a fumbling for the lamp, the bright arc of a match, then a sharper light as the chimney settled on the base and the flame steadied.

One lamp did not give much light, but Owen Frank saw the tall, thin man as he turned toward him, a short barreled gun in his hand. "Stand him up," the man said. He was near forty and his clothes were old and badly patched. A bachelor, Owen Frank thought with disjointed clarity.

The man who held Frank released him, at the same time jerking the .44 Remington from Frank's holster. When the man stepped around him, Frank saw that it was Meechum.

"You weren't so tough with Sweikert tonight," Frank reminded him, and Meechum scowled.

"Shut up," Meechum said. "I always wanted to shoot one of you, so don't give me an excuse."

"You were pretty stupid to come back up here," the man near the table said.

"So I'm stupid," Frank said dryly. "Do I get a prize?"

The man prodded him with his short barreled gun as though the temptation to shoot was so strong he could barely resist it. "Harry Showers was one of the whitest guys that ever lived."

"He was impulsive though," Frank said, and measured these men, deciding that they were dangerous now. "I asked him to leave me alone but he had something different on his mind."

"You should have left town with Alvertone's bunch," Meechum said in a deep rumble. He hefted Owen Frank's Remington. "We won't have to fight you after tonight."

Without warning he hit Owen Frank a sledging blow along the shelf of the jaw. Being completely unexpected, the power spun Frank around, driving him into the pine dresser with enough force to break it into kindling.

Bouncing from the impact, he fell. He had difficulty getting to his feet, for the left side of his face felt numb and a paralysis gripped his arms and legs.

The big man hit him again but Frank swayed away from it, taking a painful rake along the cheekbone. This had the effect of a blast of cold water. Strength poured back into him, although he acted as though he were about to fold in the middle.

Thinking he had a sure thing, Meechum stepped in. Owen Frank axed him in the stomach, bringing the man's mouth open wide in a soundless, windless cry. Whistling his fist up, Frank clacked the man's jaws together, then pulped his nose before whirling toward the man with the gun.

He understood these two now: brave when they were not faced with a gun. These were men who settled things with their fists and let it go at that.

Meechum was still against the door where Frank's blow had driven him, shaking his head and trying to get his eyes to focus. Pouncing on the other man, Frank got in a solid lick. The man ducked the next punch and whipped the gun down. Frank had been waiting for it. He seized the man's wrist, whirling him like a ball on the end of a string before releasing him to crash face first into the wall.

The fight was whetting his appetite. He laughed, a clear

19

ringing sound, and dived against Meechum as the man shuffled forward. He struck the big man twice under the heart and again in the mouth, drawing blood. When Meechum back-pedaled, Frank followed him, stabbing him again with his fist. Meechum's knees buckled.

Behind Frank, the other man was advancing. Frank whirled, bending low to drive in at his stomach. The gun descended and Frank took a numbing blow on the back before he upset the man and wrestled the gun away from him, carrying him back against the bed. The side rails gave way, dumping springs, mattress and boards to the floor with a crash.

Frank hit the man across the bridge of the nose and felt him go limp, while behind him and near the door, Meechum scrambled to his feet. Frank's breath was a ragged sawing now and sweat stung his cheek where Meechum's fist had broken the skin.

Ten feet separated him from the big man. Frank drove at him, contacting with the point of his shoulder and taking him back. When Meechum hit the door, off balance and falling, there was a loud shredding of wood and the casing came free, dumping both of them into the hall.

Grabbing his gun, which Meechum still clutched, Frank tried to gain his feet and turn. He didn't quite make it. The man with the short barreled gun banged it against the crown of Owen Frank's head and the tall Texan went down, sprawling across Meechum.

From below there came a stomp of booted feet and Will Savage's head and shoulders appeared at the head of the hall. There was not much light here, just a feeble glow cast by the small bracketed lamps.

"Dammit," Savage snapped. "What the hell do you think you're doing, Clover? Get him off Meechum!"

Slipping his gun into the waistband of his pants, Jim Clover pulled Owen Frank off his friend and helped Meechum up. A good-sized crowd had followed the sheriff up the stairs and Savage turned on them, waving them back down.

Meechum was sitting up alone now, touching his face tenderly where Owen Frank's fists had bruised it. He said, "Help me up, Jim."

He leaned heavily against the wall and pawed at the

blood dripping from his nose. Jim Clover's face was marked and a large red spot blossomed on his cheek. "You're a pretty looking pair," Savage said. "You want to enforce the law, I'll make you deputies."

Footsteps sounded on the stairs. Joanne Avery stopped beside Savage. "Somebody better help him," she said.

"What's one gunfighter more or less?" Meechum muttered, feeling his teeth to see if any were loose. He straightened and added, "You going soft? Whose side are you on, anyway?"

"That's enough of that!" Savage said sharply. "Get downstairs, both of you."

"Watch the pushing," Clover warned. "Damn it, my dander's up."

"Looks like Frank took some of it out of you," Savage said. "Go on, wait for me in the lobby."

Clover glanced at Meechum, but the big man was too sick to care where he went. He stood spraddle-legged, dabbling at the blood on his face. Some of his surliness was still evident but the fight had taken all urge for action out of him.

"By golly," he said, "a man's just got to hit out sometime. You didn't break your back to arrest him when Harry was shot." He glared at Savage as though all his troubles were the sheriff's fault.

"I don't like this any better than you do," Savage snapped. "Harry made a mistake and with all the witnesses there, no jury in the world would convict Owen Frank." He pawed his mouth out of shape. "Dammit all, tonight I thought I had Alvertone cold. Sweikert was waiting by the express office to shoot Harry when he got on the stage. It was the break I'd been waiting for."

"I got a notion to pack my things and pull out," Jim Clover said. "You wait and see, Will—when election comes around, Alvertone will see that his man wins."

"The election will go fair and square," Savage said flatly. "I'll have deputies on the street to see that there's no funny business."

Clover laughed. "Who are you going to get? Sweikert or Reilly will pick a fight and then you'll have dead deputies. One shot and they'd all scatter." He shook his head hopelessly. "Come on, Fred. Let's get back to the grove."

"That's a good idea," Savage said. "Stay near the wagon camp and stop trying to stick your nose in where it don't belong."

"What are you going to do with him?" Meechum asked dully. He looked like a bear in his heavy coat and blood-mottled face.

"I'll put him on his horse and shy him out of the country."

"Was I you, I'd be careful," Meechum warned. "He's been in the fire before and he ain't melted."

"I'll take care of my office," Savage said. "Don't give me any more trouble."

"Watch that kind of talk, Will," Clover said with deceptive softness. "Don't start shoving me around. I won't take it."

"Don't be so proud you can't take a warning," Savage told him, and leaned some of his authority against Clover, watching the man yield a little.

"Showers was the first to break from the grove," Meechum said. "Which of us will be next? It's easy for you to talk, Will. You walk around and try to keep everybody from fighting, but a man can just take so much. The land's out there and we're getting tired of waiting. One of these days we're going to leave the grove and move onto Teepee range."

"I ought to lock you both up for your own good," Savage said. "Now go on back to the grove and shut up."

"We'll move out when we get ready," Clover said. "Don't try to stop us, Will."

"You threatening me?"

"Remember what I said," Clover stated and helped his friend down the stairs.

Joanne Avery had remained quiet, for she knew Will and understood that he resented any intrusion in the administration of his office. Perhaps this was his major fault, an exactness that he himself couldn't satisfy. He tried to please everyone in the performance of his duty, a task that only a proud man would attempt.

Now she touched him on the arm and said, "Hadn't you better call the doctor, Will? He hasn't moved. He may be badly hurt."

"The devil with it," he snapped, exhibiting the frayed

ends of his temper. "Now don't start that on me, **Joanne.** You feeling sorry for him?"

She shrugged. "I don't like to see him lying there like that. Help me take him into his room."

"If you're determined to make a point of it," Will said, and took hold of Owen Frank's shoulders, dragging him into the room.

"On the bed," Joanne said. "What's left of it."

Savage looked disgusted, but he placed Owen Frank on the bed, upper body first, then his feet. Blood seeped from a crease in the tall man's scalp and Joanne Avery bent over him, looking at him for a long moment.

"I hit him," she said. "I shouldn't have done it, but I had to. Too many people were watching for me to back down."

"I'm not the only one who has pride then," Savage said with a smile.

"That's what gets us into trouble," Joanne murmured. "I saw something in his eyes, Will. He didn't want to kill Harry Showers. He was sorry about it."

"Stop thinking like that," Savage said. "There's too many of his kind around here now. Alvertone's too strong. Can't you see why I want Frank out of the country?"

"He could help you," Joanne said, her voice low and her face smooth. "No man can ride the fence forever, Will, and that's what you've been trying to do. Alvertone made the country and everyone owes him money—but that doesn't count when he starts making innocent people suffer."

He looked at her oddly. "You too, Joanne? You'd like me to be a hero, wouldn't you? You want to know what happens to heroes? They end up dead or without a shirt on their backs. Joanne, what do you expect of a man?"

She smiled faintly. "You don't really know me, do you, Will? You should. You asked me to marry you."

"Joanne—" he began, then slapped his thigh. "Being sheriff is more than arresting drunks. You want me to arrest Alvertone and tell him that he's wrong for putting forty years of his life into a land, that now he should open his arms and let these squatters camped at the grove move in on him? Joanne, get some sense. I have to play this game with a little caution and avoid antagonism."

"You think Alvertone likes that?" she asked. "Maybe

23

that's why he means to shove you out in the election week after next and put in his own man. He must have a lot of faith in your fence-straddling policy."

"I'll win the election," Savage said flatly. "There's enough homesteaders in the grove—plus the townspeople—to re-elect me."

"Will you?" She shook her head. "Let's face the facts, Will. Half the merchants have built their whole life around Teepee money. Which way are they going to fall when the ballots are cast?"

"What do you want me to do?" he asked. "What—"

"If you don't know, I'm sure I couldn't tell you," she said, and her voice was like a dry wind with no comfort in it.

He took her shoulders, pulling her around until she faced him. The lamplight fell on his face, boyishly handsome. Hair lay in blond chunks across his forehead. "I don't want to quarrel with you and it's leading to that. You're a woman and it's easy for you to tell me to go out and shoot Alvertone's gunmen."

"Right is right, and to some men that's reason enough to fight. You have to believe in it and I don't think you do. A man has to stand firm for something, Will, even if it's wrong."

"Like Owen Frank?" Savage laughed brittlely. "Comparing me to that Texas gunfighter is not very flattering, Joanne."

She slanted him a puzzled look. "Is it flattery you're looking for, or the truth?"

Owen Frank moaned and stirred and they turned to look at him. Joanne added, "Be careful, Will. Meechum and Clover no longer trust you. That's why they laid for him instead of waiting to see what you'd do. They already knew."

"So that's the way it is," he said, and some anger worked into his eyes. Swinging away from her abruptly, he went out and down the stairs. She listened to the rap of his boots and then turned to help Frank as he tried to sit up.

He sat on the wrecked bed, bent over, his head hanging down. After watching him for a minute, she went downstairs to get water. Filling a wooden bucket, she returned and stepped over the fallen door.

He stood by the commode, and when her foot crunched on the splintered wood he whirled toward her, the gun flashing from his holster. On the table, the lamp burned brightly, feeding soft light into the room and casting long shadows on the wall. Her eyes remained on the gun even after he put it away. As she had entered, her eyes had unconsciously focused on the cedar butt angling away from his hip. She had been unable to follow the slash of his hand, or the draw, for it was like the subtle wink of an eye, so fast that it had to be sensed rather than seen.

The water in the porcelain bowl became pink as Owen Frank washed the cuts on his face and head. Toweling himself dry, he said, "You come up to give me another poke in the teeth?"

"No," Joanne said. "Jim Clover hit you with his gun. Are you hurt bad?"

"It'll heal," Frank said, and winced when he touched the towel to his torn scalp. "Weren't you in here a minute ago? I thought I heard you." He waved it aside as of no consequence. "How did Meechum and Clover get in my room? You give them a key?"

"Yes."

"You're full of cute tricks, aren't you?"

"No," she said. "I liked Harry Showers and because of it I acted hastily. A lot of people liked Harry."

"But a few hated him," Frank said. "Sweikert intended to kill him. I didn't. There's a difference, you know."

"I know," Joanne said and watched him. The lamp cast deep shadows along the planes of his face.

With a disgusted motion Owen Frank tossed the towel aside and righted a chair to sit down, resting his elbows on his knees, his head dropped forward. "It was like a dream," he said in a droning voice. "The damn fool kept talking and I couldn't get to him. Then he shot. When I answered it I heard him grunt. I intended to just take his gun away when I ran out the door, but it—it was like having hold of something and not being able to let go. He kept shooting. What could I do?" He slapped his hands against his knees. "Then Sweikert came across the street, laughing." Frank shook his head and matted hair fell across his forehead. "That sheriff is worried about getting votes, isn't he?"

"He has to get them," Joanne said. "He's asked me to marry him." She studied him for his reaction.

Raising his head, Owen Frank looked at her boldly for a moment. She stood quietly, her back against the wall, a tall girl bathed in lamplight. Behind her, the long shadow reached to the ceiling. In her flowing dress her hips were slender, flaring faintly, and she seemed to have no waist at all. Her bare arms, crossed under firm breasts, were slender but suggestive of strength.

His eyes lingered on her face, and in her eyes he read her pride and a will that, like his own, knew no bending. She was a woman who would have what she wanted, but in the soft curve of her lips he read something else—a promise, perhaps, of a gentleness that she had yet to show a man. This was the contradictory thing about her and the mystery pulled at him.

"I gave you credit for having better judgment," Frank told her with brutal bluntness, but she showed no resentment. "He's short weight in the job. He'll never hold Alvertone back when the man begins to cut loose."

"I know," she murmured, and left her place along the wall. "You'd better let me fix your head. It's bleeding again."

He moved the straight-backed chair while she adjusted the lamp higher. Parting his hair, she peered at the slash and made soft clucking sounds. Pouring fresh water from the bucket, she dipped the end of the towel and bathed the wound. "Don't blame Jim and Fred Meechum for this. They've been pushed hard and now they're all jammed together down at the grove."

"That the camp at the end of town? I saw the campfires from the window."

"Alvertone won't let them go any farther," she said.

"I know," he murmured.

"Do you?" Her voice said that she didn't believe him.

"They swarmed all over my place," he said. "Others too. Got so bad with the fences that we rode on 'em. A few ran and a few got burned out. Some others fought and got killed. There's something dirty about winning in a land grab. After it was over I gave it back to the Indians and started riding."

"What's over all those hills, Owen?" She used his name naturally and it seemed right somehow.

"Nothing," he admitted. "The fun's in looking, not in the finding."

"Do you have a razor? I'll have to shave off some of the hair before I can put a bandage on that."

He made a motion toward his saddlebags and she untied the strings, dumping the contents on the bed. There was another gun in a shoulder holster, along with his soap and shaving gear. She worked up a lather with the soap. "I couldn't live like that—chasing rainbows."

"Why stay in one place?" he said. "A man has a choice. He can be free and ride in the sun. Why shouldn't he enjoy it?"

Bending his head to one side, she moved the razor in short, quick strokes, the bite of the steel against hair a soft whisper in the room. Ripping a pillowcase, she made a flat bandage and tied it over his left ear. "Keep it moist and it should heal quickly." She stood back and looked at him. "I suppose you'll be leaving now."

"Nothing to hold me here," he said, and studied his hands. "A long time ago I learned never to mix in other men's quarrels."

"Why not stay and make this one yours?" she suggested.

"Uh-uh," he said and stood up, a little shaky. "What was Harry Showers? Alvertone must have been afraid of him."

"He was just a little man," she said. "He was a fighter and he meant to buck Alvertone and his men. He was going after a United States marshal to settle this thing."

"And I ruined it," Frank said. "Along with a lot of people's hopes. I didn't want to kill him. He started shooting—" He spread his hands and let the words trail off into nothing.

"Yes," Joanne said softly. "That's how it goes. Someone starts shooting, then there's no way to stop it. For three months I've been holding my breath, waiting for the first shot, and tonight you fired it. That's the beginning. Maybe you can tell me the end."

"You're blaming me, aren't you? You think I'm a gunfighter like Sweikert and Reilly?"

"Aren't you?"

"No," he said flatly. "There's a difference. All Texans are good with a gun, girl."

"But not as good as you," she said, massaging her hands together.

Owen Frank shook his head for he had no argument. His

skull pounded with the regularity of his pulse and a sickness pulled at his stomach. Picking up his hat, he punched it into shape and found that it fitted fairly well over the bandage.

"Thanks for the free nursing," he said, and went to the door.

"Wait," she said quickly. She came over to him, moving around so she could see his face. "You're a tough man, Owen Frank, and I've been thinking about what you said —the nesters you fought in Texas. What did you see afterward that made you leave? What was there about it that was so bad that you couldn't live with it any more?"

"You saw it tonight," he said, his lips drawing tight. "Harry Showers' widow."

"Don't go," she said. "I'm after a horse trade, can't you see that?" She saw no refusal in his eyes and added, "I think you may find whatever you're searching for if you'd stop in one place long enough. I'm not asking you to fight Burk Alvertone. I just want you to stay and keep Will Savage out of it. Give him a fence to straddle."

"Seems to me," Frank said, half amused, "that you're getting the best of this."

"The woman always gets the best," Joanne said. "What you get can't be put in your pocket, but it's important or you wouldn't keep on looking."

His forehead wrinkled into a frown. "You want me to keep Will Savage from getting bruised. Are you in love with him? He won't thank you for this. No man would."

"I—I don't know any more," Joanne said. "I just don't want to see him dead. He's not able to handle Alvertone now, but some day he'll get elected for something else and it'll be all right. I just don't want to see him get trampled."

"I'll think about it," Frank said, and moved past her.

"Make a visit to the grove with me," she said. "I'll go any time you're ready."

"Maybe later." He smiled. The severity left his face. He looked younger for a moment, and slightly reckless. "You're clever," he said softly. "I'll have to remember that."

He went down the hall, shrugging into his coat. At the bottom of the landing he turned. Joanne Avery was at the head of the stairs, watching him.

CHAPTER 3

The hotel lobby was vacant as Owen Frank crossed it on his way out, but on the porch a man was waiting for him. A girl stood in the deeper shadows along the wall and Frank paused as Reilly, the young Teepee hand he'd met in the saloon, stepped across the bar of light flung from the front window.

Glancing past him, Owen Frank could barely distinguish the girl's features in the shadows. Her hair was dark, framing an oval face, and the coarse dress identified her as a homesteader.

Reilly looked over his shoulder when he caught Frank's appraisal and said, "That's Lottie Meechum. You roughed up her pappy considerable." The young man laughed softly, shook a sack of Duke's Mixture free of his shirt pocket and began rolling a cigarette.

"Burk Alvertone wants to see you right away," Reilly said, and raked a match against the hotel wall. "I'm supposed to bring you."

"I don't lead worth a damn," Frank said. "I'll come over when I get ready—if I get ready."

In the darkness, Reilly's teeth glistened as his smile widened. He drew on his smoke, the red end glowed and faded, and finally he spun it into the dust.

Watching him, Frank could see the brash pride in the man's eyes, for here was a challenge and Reilly was the kind who couldn't put one aside. Frank understood the rules for it was a game he had played many times. It never varied and he was almost pleased to see Reilly take the bait. After a thousand miles he still found it waiting wherever he stopped or whenever two men pushed against each other.

"Burk said now," Reilly said in the softest of voices. "I like to try a tough man, Frank." He laughed. "I pegged you the minute I saw you in the saloon."

"You don't want to play by my rules," Frank said. "Move on now before you buy yourself some trouble."

"When *I'm* ready," Reilly said. "I don't shove either."

"All right," Owen Frank said, and without warning his hand flashed out, fastening in the folds of Reilly's shirt. Cloth ripped sharply as Frank yanked the lighter man, nearly jerking him off his feet. Reilly's hand flashed for his gun but Frank had been ahead of him, batting the hand away and ripping the Colt free of the holster. He threw the gun and shoved Reilly backward at the same time. The Colt popped in the dusty street and Reilly went into the porch rail, his feet flying out and up as he grabbed frantically for the upright to regain his balance.

This saved him from falling and he pulled himself erect, no longer smiling. His shirt hung in tatters over his belt, with the collar and one sleeve still on.

Standing there, Owen Frank waited with a drawn-out patience. Finally Reilly shrugged and moved around the tall man, going off the porch. He hesitated by his gun as though pondering the wisdom of retrieving it, then scooped it up and continued on across the street without a backward glance.

Turning to Lottie Meechum, Frank asked, "A friend of yours?"

"Oh, no," Lottie said quickly, as though Frank had accused her of a sin. "He—he sometimes frightens me. The way he looks at me."

She stepped into the light. Her lips were full, Frank saw, and the plain dress accentuated rather than concealed her shapeliness. He could understand why Reilly would be attracted to her, for she was a woman to stir a man's thoughts until he had to tip his hand or go away wondering. It was natural that men would watch her and the man who married her would have to put up with this. Her lashes were long and her dark eyes somehow compelling. Her animated face would express her moods and thoughts. These things she could not help, but Owen Frank wondered if it was to her advantage. Winning a man would be easy for her, easier than for Joanne Avery. But where did the real worth lie? In this woman with the obvious love of life in her eyes, or the quiet one who hid herself behind a calm exterior?

"How's your father?" Frank asked.

"He wants to see you," Lottie said. "He sent me."

"He should have sent a man," Frank said. "You live at the grove?"

"All of us live there," she said. "He said he'd wait up for you." She lifted her skirts, scurrying off the porch and down the dusty street. Owen Frank watched her for a minute and then shifted his glance to find Reilly standing on the saloon porch, his head turned to follow Lottie Meechum.

When she passed the stable at the end of the street, Reilly went into the saloon, the batwings flapping idly after his passage. Walking the boardwalk, Owen Frank entered the mercantile and bought a box of .44-40 shells and filled his belt. The remainder he dumped into his coat pocket.

"There a doctor in town?" he asked the clerk.

"On Riot Street," the clerk said, eyeing Frank's bruised face. "The third house on your left."

"Thanks," Frank said, and went out.

Walking along the boardwalk, he saw Sweikert come out of the saloon across the street. He felt a sharp surprise, for he had seen Sweikert leave town after Harry Showers was killed. Sweikert followed him with his eyes until Frank rounded the far corner, and when Frank turned to look back the gunman had disappeared back in the saloon.

The street was dark. Owen Frank walked slowly with the caution of the unfamiliar until he came to a white, two story house sitting back from the street edge. Opening the front gate, he paced up the path and dropped the brass knocker against the striking plate. Through the stained glass in the door he could see a glare of light on the upstairs landing. He rapped again, watching the light rise and waver, then slowly descend the stairs in a curious, bobbing fashion. The light seemed disembodied as it stopped in the hallway. The bolt slid back and Owen Frank said, "You the doctor?"

"That's right. Come on in," the doctor said and lifted the lamp, going through the long hall to a side room. "I was upstairs reading," he said by way of explaining the darkened house. "My wife's down to the grove, nursing some sick folks."

Opening the office door, he went in, Owen Frank following him. Going around the walls, the doctor lit several lamps and then closed the door.

The room was high paneled. An operating table stood in the middle of the floor, securely bolted, with wide leather restraining straps dangling along the sides. Medicine cabinets lined one wall and on the other side of the room a small laboratory took up most of the space.

"What seems to be the trouble?" the doctor asked, studying the prominent bruises on Owen Frank's face.

"A fellow laid a gun barrel across my head and I'd like something to stop the damn pain. It beats every time my heart does."

The doctor grunted and crossed to the medicine cabinet, sorting through the various bottles of pills on a shelf. He uncorked one bottle and shook out pellets in the palm of his hand. "You're the fellow who shot Harry Showers, aren't you?"

"Yeah," Frank said, and leaned his elbows against his knees.

"Take these," the doctor said. He handed the pills to Frank, pouring him a glass of water from a pitcher. After Frank had swallowed them, the doctor said, "He was pretty well liked around here, for a newcomer. How do you feel?"

"No different," Frank said.

"Takes a while," the doctor confided, "although the stuff's pretty strong. You working for Alvertone?"

"No," Frank said. "Neither past or present."

"What about tomorrow?"

"Tomorrow I'll be gone," Owen Frank said. He stood up. "How much do I owe you?"

"Make it fifty cents," the doctor murmured, and took the coin. "I guess you're smart, getting out now. A couple of weeks from now and it won't be fun at all. Sweikert will be the law then, or at least he'll carry the badge. This will be Alvertone's town and I'll be busy picking out bullets." The doctor sighed and placed the bottle back on the shelf, closing the glass door. "Yes, the smart ones will be gone and the dumb ones will stay and get shot. But that's always the way it goes. Only a dumb man don't know when he's licked. Sometimes he wakes up and finds out he isn't licked at all—he's really won." He gave Owen Frank a careful glance. "So I'll stay on with the dumb ones."

"Good luck," Frank told him, and walked to the door.

"You better hang on to some yourself," the doctor said.

"Moving on don't stop anything, mister. Whatever you are and whatever you've got, you'll take it along with you."

Frank replaced his hat and walked down the darkened path, thinking about what the doctor had said. The opinion was not new to him, and it was true: he had carried his burden with him. But he still had a young man's hope that someday he would ride over a hill and leave it all behind, that before him would be a place where there was no need for a gun. That's when he would stop, he told himself.

Leaving the side street, Frank's boots made small puffs of dust as he crossed over, walking along the street until he came to the saloon. He shoved the batwings open. The smell of fresh sawdust and stale beer assailed him and he went to the bar, ordering a nickel beer. The drumming in his head had abated somewhat and he found that he was not as shaky as he had been.

The bartender worked the tap and slid a schooner before Frank, then began polishing a spot by the tall Texan's elbow.

Drinking deeply, Owen Frank raised a hand and brushed the foam from his mustache. Searching the room through the back mirror, he saw Burk Alvertone, Sweikert and Reilly at a corner table. Studying the swarthy gunman, Frank saw all the signs of a proud, boastful man. A fancy dresser, Sweikert wore a cartridge belt with right and left hand holsters threaded on it, both guns carried high and well forward on his thighs. The tie downs wound around his legs to be knotted on the outside. Both guns sported pearl handles, lustrous and opalescent in the lamplight.

Leaning on the bar, Owen Frank nursed the feeling that the bartender wanted to talk. Frank said, "How did business turn out after all?"

"Poor," the man said. "No hard feelings, but I was betting on the other guy."

"Showers?"

"The man had his points," the bartender said. "I like to sell beer to a farmer, mister. They drink it and don't fight. With these cattlemen I get too damn much furniture broke up. I can't afford it."

"That's the risks you take," Frank said, and smiled faintly. Finishing his beer, he pushed the glass aside and

33

crossed the room, moving around the tables until he flanked the one occupied by the three men.

Rolling a cigar between his fingers, Alvertone said, "You just love a fight, don't you?"

"Depends," Frank said. He glanced at Reilly, but the young man was studying a spot on the green velvet where someone had set a whisky glass and left a stain. Reilly's shirt still hung in tatters.

"You think it over yet?" Alvertone asked, and popped the cigar in his mouth. "I pay the going wage—seventy a month and no work. When Sweikert gets to be sheriff, he'll make you his deputy."

"I've thought it over," Frank confessed, "and I don't want it. I'm leaving in the morning and don't make any mistakes because I'll slap your damn hands if you do."

Alvertone sat absolutely motionless, his cigar smoldering and forgotten between his fingers. Reilly stopped looking at the circular stain, his eyes coming up to Frank's face.

"Brave talk," Sweikert said smugly and placed his hands flat on the table. "Don't get the idea you're doing us any favors."

Flipping his head toward the man, Frank asked, "Were you going to shoot Showers in the back tonight, or take your chances from the front?"

Alvertone's hand came out quickly and fastened on Sweikert's wrist. "Let him talk," he said, and Sweikert relaxed. Glancing at Frank, he said, "Get out of the country then, but don't wait until morning. Do it tonight."

Owen Frank laughed and walked out.

For several minutes, Burk Alvertone stared at the bat-wings, his fingers drumming on the table. To Sweikert, he said, "Take care of this and make it look good. You stay here with me, Reilly."

"I know how," Sweikert said. He pushed back his chair, going out with unhurried strides. Alvertone sat quietly, enjoying his cigar.

At last he said, "How about some casino, Reilly? You know, you really ought to get another shirt. You look like hell."

Entering the hotel lobby, Owen Frank paused at the desk. A spindly clerk sat on the high stool, reading an

34

old copy of *Harpers*. Frank said, "Which room is Joanne Avery's?"

"At the head of the stairs," the clerk said. "But she ain't there." He jerked his thumb toward a door in the back. "Her father keeps a room there. She's with him."

"Thanks," Frank murmured, and skirted the desk. Rapping lightly, he heard her heels click on the floor and entered when she opened the door, sweeping off his hat as she closed it. An old man sat by the fire, a heavy robe wrapped around legs that were thin and without strength. He turned his head to look at Owen Frank.

"This is my father, Gus," she said. "Owen Frank."

"Come around where I can get a good look at you," Gus Avery said, and Frank moved to the fireplace, leaning his shoulder against the mantel. The old man studied him with a bluntness that made Owen Frank smile a little. Finally Gus Avery grunted and said, "You'll do. Have a seat." Flipping his head around to his daughter, he added, "Fix me a cup of coffee and find my pipe."

"No coffee and no tobacco," Joanne said softly.

"Got a bad heart," Gus said and thumped his chest. "Damn thing almost quit workin' on me the other day. That fool doctor! A man's last days on earth approachin' and he can't enjoy his pipe and coffee!"

"Just a few puffs then," Joanne relented and packed it for him. Gus Avery clamped it between his teeth and she arced a match, glancing at Owen Frank while the old man drew until the bowl glowed red.

In that brief interchange Owen understood this girl completely, for in her eyes he read a courage that stirred his admiration. Gus Avery was dying, and recognizing it clearly she wasted no time on sorrow, regret or tears. Time and age were demanding that she let go of a man she loved and she faced it squarely.

"Thank you," Gus murmured when he had the pipe going. He drew in a deep lungful and coughed with a deep wracking sound. Joanne's eyes grew troubled but she erased it instantly and turned away. Owen Frank looked across the room into a large square mirror and saw her face, full of pain and grief, the emotions her pride would not permit her to reveal.

"You wanted to go down to the grove?" Owen asked, and she raised her head, meeting his eyes in the mirror.

"Yes," she said. "I'll get a shawl." She left the room and Owen went back to the mantel, his blunt fingers rolling a cigarette.

"You've seen her man," Gus said. "What do you think?"

The surprise was evident on Owen's face and the old man waved his hand. "Let's not pussyfoot—I don't have the time. He's not for her, Frank. She knows it but she's given her word and to her that means something."

"It should," Owen said.

"Agh!" Gus said. "A woman's word. Same with a man's fool promises to a woman. Was I to have held her mother to all the things she promised, and she held me to mine, we'd have strangled each other." The old man put down his pipe and leaned forward in his chair. "She's got a will of her own and her own ideas about what a man ought to be. The one she marries will be some jack rabbit. He'll have to be to tame her." He stopped talking as he heard her descend the stairs and his eyes flashed an appeal. "Help me, Frank."

"People do what they want to do," Frank said. "I can't help you." Then Joanne opened the door.

"I'm ready," she said, and he followed her out, not wanting to look at Gus Avery.

On the hotel porch he paused. She glanced at him quickly before following his eyes across the street to where Sweikert waited against the saloon wall. Looking back at Owen Frank, she saw that he understood Sweikert's intent, and understanding it, was willing to play. Danger held no fear for him; rather it came as a welcome challenge. He was a born fighter and nothing would change that for him.

In a moment, Sweikert lowered his head, allowing his wide hat brim to shield his face. In so doing he opened a valve to drain off the tension that flowed back and forth across the street. She realized that the gunman wanted a fight and that her presence had prevented it. On Owen Frank's face there was neither relief nor resentment. For him, the affair was merely postponed.

She took his arm and he responded to the signal, walking down the street with her. For some distance neither spoke. Then she said gently, "Do you have to, Owen?"

"Sweikert?" He laughed. "The man has a lot of pride and most of it is false. I think Alvertone sicked him to it. Burk told me to get out of town tonight."

"Oh," she said, and fell silent.

A night wind blew gently from the west, scuffing across the desert and the lava beds farther to the west and south. Painted Rock lay in the bend of a river, the Big Lost, as the mountain men called it. Farther east, and across a great vastness of barren land and more lava beds, lay Idaho Falls, a lively town, nestled in a bend of the Snake.

At the end of the street they stepped off the boardwalk and continued along the side of the dusty road, crossing the wooden bridge a few minutes later. Beneath them the river gurgled softly and they took a wagon road to the right.

In a wide area bracketed by a sweeping bend in the river, the homesteaders had made their camp, surrounded by cedar and pine. Most of the brush had been cleared away and the wagons were scattered among the trees, the cookfires glowing brightly in the night.

Pausing at the outer rim of the camp, Joanne said, "Fred Meechum is the leader. We'll go to his wagon first."

"All right," Frank agreed, and walked with her across the compound. As they had approached the camp, he had been aware of the blended murmur of voices, the shriller pipings of children at play. But when they stepped past the first wagon, a hush started to settle over the area, and by the time they had gone halfway across there was complete silence. Several of the farmers left their families and followed Owen and the girl. The procession grew until there were twenty men behind them. Joanne stopped by a high-sided lumber wagon.

On the ground beside the fire, Fred Meechum lay on his blankets, a wet cloth over his face. An older woman washed the supper dishes, looking up in surprise as she saw Joanne Avery and Owen Frank. Lottie came from the wagon and spoke softly to her mother, who put down the pan and hurried off.

"How are you feeling, Meechum?"

Owen Frank's voice had the effect of a bayonet stab. Meechum snatched off the cloth and made a sprawling dive for the shotgun which leaned against the wagon wheel. Kicking out, Owen sent the weapon spinning, and a dull mutter went up from the men gathered close behind him.

"Wait!" Lottie shouted, and her voice held them for a moment.

"You said you wanted to see me," Owen Frank said. "What for? To shoot me?" He turned his back to the man

37

and took two tin cups from the stack of dishes, pouring coffee for himself and Joanne. His cool disregard for Meechum had its effect and the men shifted their feet, no longer sure about this tall man with the calm eyes.

"I'll get you something to sit on," Lottie said nervously. She brought out a folding stool for Joanne. Squatting, Owen Frank nursed his cup of coffee, raising his head as Will Savage pushed through the gathering.

"What are you doing here?" he asked Frank. Then he saw Joanne sitting by the wagon wheel. "I see," he added. "Joanne, I'd like to talk to you."

"All right," she said agreeably. She finished her coffee, rose, and left with Will Savage. Around Meechum's wagon a thick silence descended.

Owen drank his coffee and shied the grounds into the fire. Rolling a smoke, he reached for a long twig for his light. Over the flame, he looked at Meechum and said, "You're pretty well set up. Good plow. The wagon's sound. Seems that a man as careful as you would know better than to come into cattle country."

"We didn't know," Meechum said, and wiped his bruised face with the cloth. One eye was completely closed and his lips were two raw rolls of flesh. High on his cheekbone, the skin was split and faintly bleeding.

"I'm from Illinois," Meechum continued. "An agent from a land company came around with folders advertising all the free land out here. Later, I sold out and headed West. The fella never said anything about cattlemen using the land. We didn't come here for trouble."

"But now you're here and you've got it," Frank said. "You goin' back?"

"To what?" Meechum asked. "No. None of the others either."

Frank turned and looked at the men ringing him. They were stern-faced, bluntly honest men who had worked hard for everything they owned. There was no friendliness in their eyes for him, but neither was there an open animosity. He understood them, the patient, waiting kind who had to be sure before they did anything.

He had seen these faces before on other men who had moved onto his land in Texas. The same patient, dogged breed who loathed trouble and had more than their share of it. He had killed men like them, he and other cattlemen who had banded together to drive them out.

Owen Frank lowered his eyes and kicked a stick of wood into the fire. Meechum's voice pulled his attention around.

"Why did you come here?"

"Your daughter asked me to," Frank said. "You're thinking of something. What is it?"

"I just wanted to see if you had enough nerve to come into this camp after killing Harry Showers."

"Don't make up stories," Frank said. "You know damn good and well I shot Showers in self-defense. Your daughter told you what happened to Reilly. You're not going to hurt me, Meechum. You're not sure where I stand yet."

"Ugh," Meechum grunted and looked around at the other farmers. He singled one man out, a rail-thin man with a gaunt face. "What do you think, Rogers?"

"I don't cuddle up to no gunfighter," Rogers said, and spat a stream of tobacco onto the ground.

"Harris?"

"I'll reserve judgment," he said, shifting his big-boned frame.

"I'm worried," Meechum admitted. "Will Savage is coming up for re-election in two weeks. The cattlemen are going to see that he don't get it."

"Not my worry," Owen Frank said. "I'm drifting."

A defeated expression washed over Meechum's face and he made an idle, futile motion with his hand before letting it drop in his lap.

"Thanks for the coffee and talk," Owen Frank told him, and stood up. "I hope you make out all right."

"You hope. But you don't believe it."

"That's right," Frank said honestly, and parted the men to break free and cross the compound.

Glancing around, he saw the women and children watching him, for the combined firelight made the center of the wagon park bright. He looked at their faces and then looked away quickly for there was too much worry there.

From across the park he saw Joanne Avery and walked toward her. Will Savage was nowhere in sight and he wondered about this. He touched her arm and he said, "Ready to go back?"

"If you are."

"Where's Will?"

"He went back to town," Joanne said. She took his arm and they walked slowly out of the camp. The wind rustled the trees and the night held a peace of its own.

"Will is afraid to trust you," she said.

"I didn't ask him to trust me," Frank said. "I'm leaving in the morning, Joanne."

"Oh," she said softly. "I had hoped you'd stay. I tried hard enough, didn't I?"

"Very hard," he admitted. "I saw what you wanted me to see in the grove. The same faces, the same worry making the women old before their time. Sorry, Joanne—it's not my fight at all."

"I guess it isn't." She sighed. "There's lots of hills to the north for a man to ride over. I hope you find what you're looking for."

"Am I hunting anything? I thought I was just baying at the moon."

"You've convinced yourself of that," she said. "I wouldn't try to argue you out of it. But there's going to come a time when you'll tire of it and start looking back. All you'll see is a string of towns and a lot of hills. You won't even be able to remember where they were."

In his mind he thanked her silently for not saying the things she could have said about his leaving now. She would have little hope for the future. The farmers would talk and curse their plight, but there was no real fight in them. They needed a fighter to lead them. Will Savage would be of no use, for Alvertone was sure to bully the election around to suit himself.

He wondered how far he would get down the road before Gus Avery died. The thought shocked him and he knew what he would remember best: that brief glimpse of her face in the square mirror. He wondered if he would ever forget it.

They went the rest of the way in silence, for there was nothing more either of them could say. He had his own star to follow and she was too proud to beg.

On the hotel arcade, he hesitated to scan the street. There was no sign of Sweikert, but Owen Frank knew that the man had not given up. Joanne read this in his face and murmured, "But you would fight *him*, wouldn't you?"

"A personal matter," he said.

"I see," she said, and there was a coolness in her voice, breaking past her reserve. "Goodnight, Owen—and good luck."

She went inside. He watched her through the window as she mounted the stairs, and when she passed from his sight, he felt a sharp sense of loss.

CHAPTER 4

After the second hand of casino, Reilly pushed the cards away from him and said, "I think I'll go buy me another shirt."

He glanced around the saloon, finding it bare. Felix was washing down the beer taps, paying no attention to Burk Alvertone and the young gunfighter. When Alvertone made no objection, Reilly pushed back his chair and walked out.

Near the door, Sweikert leaned against the wall. He favored Reilly with a quick nod and asked, "Where you goin'?"

"To get me a new shirt."

Sweikert laughed and an unpleasant light crept into his eyes. "No man would ever do that to me." He grinned at Reilly but there was no humor in it. Reilly and the heavy man had come from the same part of Texas, but Reilly felt no kinship with him. There was something dark about the man's mind that Reilly couldn't define. Sweikert's eyes made him uncomfortable. They reflected an utter absence of emotion even when he laughed.

The young man thought of Owen Frank's eyes, remembering the inner sadness mirrored in their depths, a compassion that made them seem incredibly old.

Swinging away, Reilly crossed the loose dust and entered the mercantile. Working his way past the hanging harness, the barrels and boxes of goods, he stopped by the clothing counter and sorted through the shirts. He found a red and white plaid his size and bought it for a dollar, using the back room to change.

Before he threw the ripped shirt away, he frowned at it

for several minutes, vividly recalling the quick rip of the cloth and the dangerous moments following it. Why hadn't he picked up his gun and shot at Owen Frank? That was his job, wasn't it? Remembering, he knew suddenly that he really didn't want to shoot a man.

Pitching the ragged shirt into the alley, Reilly went back through the store and out to the street. He paused on the boardwalk, glancing up and down, seeing Sweikert still by the saloon wall.

He took out his tobacco and fashioned a cigarette. Then he cut across the street and navigated the crack between two buildings. Once in the alley, he broke into a run, emerging on a cross street that was little more than a lane.

The night was inky black here, leaving him only his instincts to trust for direction. Reaching the end of the lane, Reilly struck off through the brush at an angle until he reached the river. The Big Lost was not wide here and he walked easily along the bank, sheltered from sight by the dark and the overhanging branches of willows.

At last he came to a large pine deadfall that formed a foot bridge. He waited for a moment, listening, then crossed over. Now he was close to the farmers' wagon camp in the grove. Staying clear, he moved along the bank for thirty or forty yards before hunkering down to wait.

He listened idly to the murmur of voices from the grove, relaxing a little with the sound of it. For the moment, he tried not to think of the possibility of his having to kill some of these men. Without knowing why, he always backed up from that thought.

Admitting it to himself, he knew that it was the lure of a gunman's wage and not the profession itself that appealed to him. Suddenly he sat bolt upright, aware of the cessation of sounds in the grove. All the voices had died abruptly and he pondered the reason.

Forcing himself to sit still, he waited patiently. There had been no sound of shooting from Painted Rock so he was reasonably certain that Sweikert had not yet met Owen Frank. Finally, the sound of voices began to drift from the grove again, carried along on the night wind. Reilly leaned back against the bole of a tree, concentrating on the night noises around him.

Ten minutes later he heard a rustling in the bushes and

the shadowy shape of a girl stepped out. "Here," Reilly called softly, and Lottie Meechum changed direction.

She knelt on the ground beside him. "Reilly, you must get out of here."

"I'm glad you came," he whispered. "I was afraid you wouldn't."

"I shouldn't have," Lottie said. "I should have told my father and had some men here to grab you." She bent closer to peer at him in the darkness. "You're a bold one, aren't you?"

"That's my stock in trade," Reilly admitted. He could smell the clean scent of soap on her skin and battled an urge to touch her. He had spoken to her on impulse while she waited for Owen Frank at the hotel. After the first few words, his natural courage had asserted itself and he had asked for this rendezvous.

That was the way of a man, he decided. He could look just so long and then he had to reach out and touch.

"What do you want?" Lottie asked, a little afraid of him and yet drawn by a force that she couldn't resist. Even in the darkness, she could trace in her mind the clean line of his jaw and the flash of his eyes, as quick as the slash of a knife. From the beginning she had read the interest in his eyes and hated the impossible barrier between them. There was a restlessness in him that matched her own.

"Just wanted to talk to you," Reilly said. "I never had a girl, not even back in Texas."

"Your kind has lots of girls," Lottie scoffed.

"What kind am I?" Reilly asked. "I don't know that myself."

"You don't belong with Sweikert and Alvertone," she said. "You could get out if you wanted to."

"You don't understand," he said hopelessly. "There's no getting out. Once I turned away from Alvertone, Sweikert would be after me. I know him, Lottie. There's no let-up in him." Reilly drew a long breath and eased it out. "I know now how Alvertone thinks. He wanted Owen Frank to come in with him, but he turned him down. Sweikert's waiting on the street in Painted Rock to shoot Frank down. He'd do that to me too, if he had to."

"Frank's in the grove with Joanne Avery," Lottie said. "I just saw him. He was talking to my father and the others."

"He coming in on your side?"

She shook her head, her braids stirring. "I don't think so. He could, but he won't. There's nothing holding him in any one place, like there is me. I wish I was like that—free to go where I wanted when I wanted. You can't do that when you owe something to someone. I guess that's why you stay, Reilly."

"I'd leave now if you'd leave with me," he told her. "I mean it, Lottie. I'd go."

"There wouldn't be any life for either of us that way," she said. "You'd spend all your time looking back over your shoulder and I'd be crying because I left my folks when I should have stayed."

"I—I like you a lot, Lottie. I'm not just sayin' that."

"I know," she whispered. "Why do you think I came here?" He bent toward her but she placed a hand on his chest. "No, Reilly. Let's just leave it like this between us, shall we? I wish it could be different."

"Then I'll have to make it different," he said with a great deal of positiveness. "Go on back to the grove and tell them that you heard Sweikert is out to kill Owen Frank. Tell them to get uptown and line the streets. Maybe it can be stopped."

She sat there for a moment, staring at him in the dark, and he took her arms, shaking her. "Girl, he's fast—awful fast—and he don't care how fair anything is. Go on now. I'll get back and see what I can do to warn Frank."

"All right," she said uncertainly, and stood up, her dress rustling. "Reilly—be careful."

"Sure," he said, and watched her be swallowed up by the foliage. He retraced his path across the deadfall and down the lane, and traveled half the length of the alley. Moving cautiously between the buildings, Reilly waited, concealed by the shadows but commanding a clear view of the street.

He saw no sign of Sweikert and this set up a vague worry in his mind, for he would have preferred to keep him in sight. Turning his head, he saw a flash of movement on the bridge and identified Joanne Avery and Owen Frank. They walked slowly to the end of the street and along the opposite boardwalk to the hotel arcade. There they stopped. Finally the girl went inside. Frank watched her until she disappeared from view. Then he walked idly down the street, looking in store windows as if he were any rider visiting town for the first time in two months.

A man's first night in a strange town is always accompanied by a feeling of unease and Owen Frank's was magnified by the flurry of violence that had occurred earlier. There was no hint of friendliness in Painted Rock, nor trust either. The two factions pulled at each other until a man was afraid to speak for fear that today's friend might turn out to be tomorrow's enemy.

Hesitating at the end of the street, Owen Frank noticed several farmers crossing the bridge. Puzzled at seeing them enter town at this hour, he was even more amazed by the fact that some carried shotguns, nestled in the crook of their arms.

Stepping into the dust, Owen Frank crossed over, walking slowly down the other side. He passed the saloon and paused before the hardware store, standing close to the window to study the merchandise. More farmers came across the bridge, infiltrating along the street until there were fifteen or twenty of them.

Owen Frank turned his head slightly to watch them, wondering what was going on. The front of this building, like most of the others on the street, was flush with the boardwalk. The door was heavy pine and the windows many foot-squares of glass.

A restlessness nudged at him as he scanned the street, watching the farmers, but they seemed to be paying little attention to him.

From the gap between the buildings a voice spoke sharply: "Heads up!" Frank looked around and found Sweikert teetering on the edge of the saloon porch.

Something in the man's stance held Owen Frank motionless. Then, in the slow movement of Sweikert's head, he detected the telltale searching of a wolf after prey. Light spilled from the doorway behind Sweikert, outlining the big man clearly, fragments of it sparkling on the pearl-handled guns. And at last he saw Owen Frank.

Sweikert stepped down to the street level and halted.

The action was like a shouted warning. Owen Frank moved a few steps along the walk until he again fronted the hardware store. Shifting a little, Sweikert stepped under

45

the hitchrail toward the center of the dusty street. Along both sides men waited silently, their presence a weight against Sweikert, driving caution through him. Walking slowly, Owen Frank paced the distance separating them and stopped on the saloon side of the hitchrail, letting the horizontal bar lie between them.

On Sweikert's face there was no clue to his temper; only his eyes were alive and watchful.

"You've been waiting for me a long time," Frank said easily. "You don't have to wait any longer, do you?"

Laughing softly, Sweikert hooked a thumb in his shell belt. Diagonally across from them, the hotel door stood open, shafting yellow lamplight onto the dust. Joanne Avery stepped out on the porch, lifting her face to feel the cool night air. She saw Frank and the gunman, and immediately read their full purpose.

Sweikert saw Frank's eyes flick across the street. He turned his own head slowly, keeping watch on Frank until the last moment, then swinging for his look and darting back.

"She's pretty," Sweikert said in a low voice. "Too good for that damned sheriff. Someday I'm going to kill him."

The farmers were waiting tensely now, bunched in a solid knot across the street. Frank said, "You pretty good at killing?"

A smile twisted Sweikert's lips. "Pretty good." He stepped forward and laid one hand on the horizontal hitchrail. "You can see how it is, Owen. You got to go. No hard feelings. I've seen tough ones like you before when they got their nose out of joint. Alvertone can't afford to fight you. Some of these earthbreakers would see it and get bold."

"So you're going to push me out, is that it?" Frank wondered fleetingly what made men do things like this. In the morning he intended to ride on, but Alvertone wasn't satisfied with that. It had to be his way and it had to be now. There was nothing stopping him except his own stubbornness. He'd go when he got ready and damn the man who told him otherwise.

"Why not?" Sweikert asked. "I see we've got plenty of witnesses." He nodded toward the farmers across the street. "Out in the rocks wouldn't be near as good. Those dirt pushers will see this and get scared. Make 'em think twice before they get ideas that Alvertone's ready to topple over. You follow me?"

"I'm way ahead of you," Frank said, and smiled. "Remember the witnesses now, Sweikert. How are you going to get me to draw first?"

The man's lip ends pulled down for a moment. "Maybe you'd reach if I belted you across the chops. Would you?"

"Try it," Frank invited, and waited, his hands hanging limp at his sides.

Raising his hand, Sweikert brushed at his mustache, then sent out a whipping blow. Owen Frank pulled his head back and reached out, imprisoning the man's wrist.

With Sweikert on the other side of the hitchrail, Frank twisted until the elbow joint was locked. Then he ducked under the bar, hauling the gunman's arm with him. Sweikert cried out when the bar caught him in the back of the arm muscle. Suddenly his feet lifted and he flew over the rail to land face down in the dust on the other side.

In a flash Owen Frank landed with both feet in the small of Sweikert's back, driving the wind from him in a long whoosh. Jerking the pearl-handled guns free of the holsters, he sailed them blindly away from him and heard them hit the boardwalk on the other side.

When Frank came erect he brought Sweikert with him. He bent Sweikert against the hitchrail and drove his fist flush in the man's face. Sweikert was without strength and made no attempt to defend himself. Methodically, Owen Frank hammered him in the face, the dull, pulpy thuds carrying along the street like rocks thrown into a stagnant pool.

When he finished, Frank stepped back, releasing the pressure against Sweikert's arched back. The man whipped forward like a freed spring and fell unmoving in the dust.

This was something the farmers could understand, a man whipping another with his fists. Before, Sweikert's guns had always held them in fear, not because they were cowards but because their lives had not been built around the use of guns. With fists they were a match for any man and Owen Frank's sound beating of Sweikert put new hope in their eyes.

Owen Frank stepped into the saloon. At the rear table, Burk Alvertone still sat, with his cigar now reduced to a

47

sour stub. The back door opened and Reilly edged inside, leaning his back against the wall.

Looking at him, Frank said, "How's it going to be, Reilly?"

"I'm out of it," Reilly said. "That was the big gun out on the street."

Alvertone stared at Owen Frank, then reached up to unbutton his coat.

"Pull it," Frank said, "and I'll blast you right out of that chair."

The ready alertness on Alvertone's seamed face changed to worry. Frank crossed the room and stood with his thighs pressed against the edge of the table.

"Your boy's out front," Frank said. "Only he don't know it right now."

Alvertone coughed slightly. "Dead?" he asked.

"No," Frank said, and his lips pulled flat and tight against his teeth. Here before him was a man who represented something that he had once been himself and now hated. "When I hit this town, I was footloose and free, but because of you I had to kill a man who never did me a bit of harm. Since then I've got beat up and cussed at because of you and now I just had one of your pet dogs sicked onto me." Frank leaned forward, his hands flat on the table. "It's high time you left town yourself—the hard way."

For a second neither moved. Then Alvertone made a desperate attempt to rise. Frank surged against the table, driving the man into the corner and spilling the table on top of him.

Under his coat Alvertone carried a short-barreled gun. He tried to get at it, but the tangle of upended table and splintered chair hindered him. Sweeping the litter away with a brisk shove, Frank grabbed Alvertone by the coat front and pulled him erect. As the man came forward, Frank snapped his head back with a stinging slap across the mouth.

By the wall Reilly waited, his hands outstretched and flat against the paneling. He made no move to assist Alvertone.

The gun Alvertone had groped for came clear of his coat. He swung it around toward Frank, but Reilly left the wall in a lunge, kicking out, and the gun whirled from Alvertone's hand. It thudded against the far wall, struck on the hammer and went off, bouncing on the sawdust covered

48

floor from the recoil. The bullet puckered the ceiling and the sudden report rang in the room like the stroke of a gong.

Without hesitation, Owen Frank raised his knee into the man's groin and Alvertone forgot about the gun. A sickly pallor spread over his cheeks and his eyes turned glassy like those of a dog in pain. His shirt was torn and his hat fell off, rolling on the floor like a loose wheel, following an ever increasingly smaller circle until it stopped.

Frank hit him again, this time with his doubled fist, and Alvertone's hair fluffed up in the back from the impact. Kicking free of the debris around his feet, Frank yanked the man from the corner and propelled him toward the door.

The bartender stood open-mouthed as Owen Frank used Alvertone's lowered head as a battering ram to rock open the swinging doors. On the street, the farmers crowded close to see this.

Alvertone was still conscious and bellowing like a mad bull. Frank stopped suddenly at the porch edge and gave him a lifting shove. The shove cascaded Burk Alvertone into the hitchrail. The hitchrail splintered under the impact and cast Alvertone into the dust by the unconscious Sweikert.

Owen Frank stood there, his legs spread, swaying like a tall tree in a whipping wind. A deadly temper possessed him and when he looked at the farmers standing there, he really didn't see them at all. He was remembering another time and other men like Burk Alvertone.

"There's the man you're all afraid of!" he shouted, pointing. "Take a good look at him with blood on his face! You see anything about him that's hard to whip? The other men who work for him are just hard working men like yourself. With the odds two to one, can't you whip the Teepee outfit?"

Without waiting for an answer he left the porch and roughed his way through the gaping farmers. On the hotel veranda he turned to watch Burk Alvertone struggle to his feet. The rancher's face was bleeding badly and his clothes were torn and fouled with dust. At the moment he looked like a dirty old man who had spent the night in the gutter because he didn't know any better. Almost blindly, Alvertone stumbled down the street toward the stable. He ignored

Sweikert completely as the gunman stirred and tried to rise.

Moving closer to Frank, Joanne Avery studied him in the lamplight flooding the open doorway. The planes of his face were set and unmoving as he watched Sweikert pull himself to his feet. Only in the expression around his eyes could she read what he felt. She saw a faint regret there, and some pity, for deep within this man the capacity for gentleness was stronger than violence.

At the far corner, Sheriff Will Savage left his office and hurried along the darkened street toward them. Rapping his toe against one of Sweikert's guns, he cursed, then picked it up. He found the other gun a moment later.

Across the street, Sweikert was having a hard time of it. Frank's fists had closed both of his eyes, blinding him effectively. Groping, Sweikert came to a portion of the hitchrack that was still standing, then stumbled and fell heavily, rapping his head solidly against the post.

A ripple of laughter went up from the farmers, swelling until it reached a full-bellied roar. Joanne saw an outraged sympathy come into Owen Frank's face, but he made no move to leave the hotel porch.

Sweikert's face was bloody and he was a hurt animal, but no one offered to help him. From the saloon, Reilly came out to stand against the wall. Perhaps he intended to help Sweikert but there were twenty farmers around the man.

Savage came on, his feet thumping the boardwalk. Spotting Owen Frank, he said, "Did you do that?" and pointed to Sweikert.

Frank regarded the sheriff with no expression at all. "Are you really stupid," he said, "or is it an act?"

Will Savage glanced around quickly to see who had heard this. His lips compressed a little. "Go back into the hotel, Joanne. This is no place for you."

"I rather like it out here," she said. "In fact I think the town's beginning to liven up."

Several of the farmers were having a little fun with Sweikert across the street. One man took Sweikert's arm and turned him, heading him off in the wrong direction. Sweikert tripped over the edge of the boardwalk. Then another farmer took him, guiding him toward a friend whose conveniently outthrust foot sent him blundering into the watering trough.

When Frank saw this his eyes filled with anger. "Let him alone!" he called, and several farmers whipped their heads around, an open belligerence on their faces.

"What the hell," one farmer said. "He's shoved us around enough times."

"I said let him alone!"

Realizing too late that he should have stopped this himself, Will Savage tried to work it out on Frank. "You're not giving the orders in Painted Rock, my friend. Better get that through your head."

"Get out of here," Frank said softly, and swayed toward Savage.

The man took an involuntary backward step before checking himself. Looking at Joanne, he saw no sympathy on her face, and this stung him. Like most proud men, he was eager to blame the other fellow for his own weakness.

"By God, now," Savage said. "I've been keeping Alvertone and these plowmen apart and now you have to break it wide open. Dammit, Alvertone will come back with his whole crew behind him!"

"Get out of here," Frank repeated. He put a hand against the sheriff's chest, shoving gently.

Across the street, the farmers had abandoned their game with Sweikert. One man took pity on the gunman and led him off toward the stable as Alvertone tore from the arch in a livery buggy, whipping it around the far corner and out of town. The drum of the running horses filtered back in fluctuating throbs carried on the night breeze.

Standing where Owen Frank had shoved him, Will Savage tried to whip up his resentment to the point of action, but somehow he could not quite carry it off. The farmers had turned their attention to Reilly, now that Sweikert was gone. They had no real grievance against the young man, aside from the fact that he was on Alvertone's payroll, but their thirst for revenge was aroused. Eight of them mounted the porch and surrounded Reilly.

Suddenly there was a lunging of bodies. Reilly was disarmed and seized by a dozen rough hands. Someone set up a cry for tar and feathers and a bedlam arose as others took it up.

Without glancing around to see if he had the sheriff's backing, Frank left the hotel porch and ran across the street, battering his way through the milling throng until he reached to Reilly.

"Let him go!" he shouted, and the calling for tar and feathers died out abruptly. "I said, let him go," Frank repeated in a soft voice, and everyone heard it.

They complied, all but one man with a thick beard and stubborn eyes who said, "Damned if I will. We'll run our own business."

"Not tonight," Owen Frank said. He hit the man, sending him sprawling into the arms of his friends. A resentful growl went up, but Frank stared at each of them, his face cool and unruffled. "Get something straight," he said. "You can't wipe your own noses. If you could, you'd have land by now and a cabin started for the winter that's only three months away. Go on back to the grove where you belong. *Go on!*"

The blast of his words turned them, one at a time, but once the tide began to break there was no stopping it until they were all walking toward the bridge. They had courage but no leader, no one to take the initiative and push their fight.

Straightening his clothes, Reilly said, "Thanks, Owen. That puts us even, don't it?"

"Even but not finished," Frank said. "You're through with Alvertone. You know that, don't you?"

"I'm through, period." Reilly fashioned a cigarette. "You think these plowpushers will trust me now, either?"

"They're to the point where they have to trust something," Frank said. Glancing across the street, he saw Savage wheel and stalk back to his office, Sweikert's pearl-handled gun dangling from a crooked finger. "What made you do it, Reilly?"

The young man shrugged, thinking of Lottie Meechum's soft voice in the darkness. "A whim," he said. "Just a whim." He drew deeply on his cigarette and shied it into the street where it hit with a scattering of sparks. "I'd like to throw in with you, Owen. It's my only chance now."

"What makes you think I'm staying?" Frank asked.

"That was your flag you just planted," Reilly said, and grinned. "I dug the hole for you by standing against the wall. I got you figured now, Frank—proud and tough. You can't pass up a good fight. You might try, but a hundred miles from here you'd stop and wonder how it came out.

The not knowing would bother you and you're the kind of fella that don't like nothin' to bother him."

"You sure you're only twenty?" Frank asked. Reilly walked across the street with him and Frank paused on the hotel porch.

Joanne Avery was still waiting. She said, "You can be a hard man, Owen Frank." Then she smiled and her reserve broke, revealing her warmth. "Come inside, both of you. I'll fix you something to eat."

CHAPTER 5

Had anyone been able to read Will Savage's thoughts, he would have found the mind complex, and the sheriff himself a curious combination of hero and coward, fool and wise man.

Sweikert's pearl-handled guns lay on Will Savage's desk and he stared at them as though they held some symbolism for him. As a matter of fact they did, for in Sweikert's hands they became a force with which he was unable to cope.

Now that they were out of Sweikert's hands their magic was dissipated, leaving them as only an exceptionally fine pair of nickel-plated .45 Colts. Opening the center desk drawer, Savage slid them inside and locked it, dropping the key in his pocket. Blowing out the lamp, he took his hat and coat from the hook and went out, walking rapidly toward the stable at the end of Buffalo Street.

The doctor was there, hitching his team of bays to his leather topped buggy. A storm lantern hung on a stanchion, pooling light over the straw-covered dirt floor. Glancing up as Savage entered, the doctor said, "Hello, Will. How bad was Alvertone hurt?"

"Banged up in the face a little," Savage said, and took his saddle down from a stall partition. "Sweikert's the one who's bad off. Frank really hurt him."

"Felix came over from the saloon and told me about it," the doctor said. "You going out there?"

"Yes. Want me to ride with you?"

"Go on ahead, if you're in a hurry," the doctor said, bending over to hook his double trees.

Tightening the cinch, Savage mounted with a dry squeaking of leather. Walking his horse to the door, he halted and asked, "Harbison, what's going to happen?"

Doc Harbison pursed his lips and shifted his glasses up on the bridge of his nose. "Don't you know, Will? Or don't you want to think about it?"

"I guess I know," Savage said dispiritedly, and raked his horse with his spurs. He pounded over the wooden bridge and left the town of Painted Rock behind him.

Ahead of him and running north and south was the Lost River Range, a string of mountains that stretched up until their tops were lost in the whips of clouds passing overhead. The valley Savage now rode through was Teepee land and an hour later he splashed through a shallow creek and turned north into a yet wider valley, carpeted with deep grass and fringed on both sides by thick stands of timber.

He could understand why Alvertone wanted to hold this range. It was cow heaven. Also, it was rich farm land with plenty of water and heavy snows to shove back the threat of drought. This land had never been turned by a plow and was rich from a thousand years' fallowing.

And all of it was Teepee land, for long ago Alvertone had crowded off the other cattlemen, controlling this valley with his crew for a distance of thirty-seven miles.

There were few ranches in this wild country. The settlers in Idaho preferred the Snake River Plains, shunning the barren lands that separated it from the wild mountain regions to the north, and in this panhandle that's all there was—mountains, never ending, rising higher and rougher with each mile.

Another hour passed before Will Savage raised the lights of Burk Alvertone's ranch. Approaching, he saw the heavy outline of the barn and corrals against the night. The house was log and rambling, set away from the other buildings which consisted of an enormous bunkhouse and scattered outbuildings.

As Savage drew near the house, a rider armed with a Spencer rifle detached himself from the shadows and said, "That's far enough. Get down and let's have a look at you."

"Put that damn gun away, Ace," Savage said, and stepped down from the saddle, moving into the light so the man could recognize him. When the muzzle of the Spencer lowered, Savage asked, "Where's Burk?"

"In the house," Ace said.

"Doc Harbison's coming behind me in the buggy. Don't take a shot at him." Savage took the porch steps two at a time and let himself in the door. Inside, a wide hall opened up into six large rooms.

Alvertone was in the main living room, almost hidden in a huge chair. He had a damp cloth over his face and beside him was a bowl of pink water.

Hearing Savage's spurs drag on the hard floor, he took the cloth away from his face and barked, "Get the hell out of my house!"

"Sorry about this, Burk," Savage said. "I was in my office and didn't hear a damn thing until it was all over. Doc Harbison's right behind me in his buggy."

"The son of a bitch!" Alvertone growled, then dabbed at his split lip. "The next time I see that Texan it's going to be over a rifle barrel."

"Not while I'm sheriff," Savage said softly. "I came out to tell you, Burk—let this pass."

Alvertone sat up straight and the pain made him wince. "Let it pass! You got a damn gall coming here with that. You think I can let Frank live and lead them farmers?"

"He's not leading the farmers," Savage told him. "He's drifting." He took a chair across from Alvertone, turning his hat brim around in his hands. Outside, someone shouted and a buggy wheeled into the yard. A moment later Doctor Harbison came into the room, taking off his coat and opening his black leather bag.

"That's quite a face you have there, Burk," he said. "Will, let me have that chair. Thank you." He moved the lamp around so it shed light on Alvertone's face and made a quick examination.

For ten minutes conversation lagged while Harbison repaired the damage. Finally the doctor closed his bag and went out, crossing the yard to the bunkhouse where Sweikert lay.

Alvertone gave Savage a venomous look and said, "I'm sick of you, Will, and I'm going to get rid of you." He hit his chest with his fist. "I made this damn country and I made the town of Painted Rock. Teepee money built every stick that stands and don't you think it didn't."

"Now you're going outside the law to make trouble for these farmers," Savage said. "That's no good, Burk. Just leave it lay. I'll do my best to keep them quiet and with winter coming on, they'll pull out. But I want it done with no bloodshed, you understand?"

"I *don't* understand," Alvertone said. "This coming election I'll own the law as well as the town."

"We'll see after election," Savage said. "Right now I want this thing carried no further. I can handle Frank. You keep your men here and we'll have no trouble."

"You're not running Teepee," Alvertone snapped. He walked to the front window, raised it and bellowed into the yard. A moment later Ace came in, still carrying his Spencer rifle. "Get Doc back in here," Alvertone ordered.

"He's still working on Sweikert," Ace said.

"Did you hear what I said?"

"Yeah," Ace said, and went out and across the yard. A few minutes later he reappeared with Doctor Harbison.

"What do you want, Burk?" Harbison asked impatiently. "That man is in bad shape. He needs working on."

"Do it then," Alvertone snarled. Glancing at Ace, he added, "Tell Rankin to get the crew together. We're riding to town."

"I said no!" Savage barked.

"And I said you're not running Teepee," Alvertone reminded him. "Get going, Ace."

"Right away, boss." The man let the door slam behind him.

"You'd better cool off, Burk," Harbison said, watching the old man closely. Alvertone's face showed a high temper and he began to pace around the room, unable to stand still.

"Mind your pills!" Alvertone told the doctor. "Savage, you're staying here. Doc, get out to the bunkhouse and fix Sweikert up proper. I'll be along with the sheriff here as soon as my men pull out."

"You can't sack the grove because of what one man did to you," Harbison said. "You're going off half-cocked, Burk. I won't let you do it."

"Better listen to me, Harbison," Alvertone warned. "I can get another doctor in Painted Rock without too much

56

trouble. If you want to practice medicine there, do as I tell you, when I tell you."

"So that's how it is." Harbison glanced at Will Savage. "So one man is ruling the country now, just like a king." He shook his head from side to side. "You've gone power crazy, Burk. Somebody ought to put you away."

Savage moved a little and Alvertone flipped his head around. "Don't try anything, Will. One yell and you won't have to wait for the election."

"Let's see if we will," Savage said, and closed the distance in one jump. Seizing Alvertone around the neck, he bent over, holding the struggling man in the crook of his arm. With his right hand he drew his revolver and pressed it into Alvertone's ear.

"Open your damn mouth now," Savage said with desperate softness, "and I'll scatter your brains all over the wall." Raising his eyes to Harbison, he said, "Take a look out of the front window and see where the crew is."

Moving the curtains aside, Harbison peered out. "By the corral. They're saddling up."

"Open the door for me," Savage said. He began to sweat. Lamplight glistened on the beads of moisture on his forehead and he felt it run down his sides beneath his shirt.

"You're cutting it pretty thin," Harbison muttered, and glanced at Burk Alvertone. Savage's grip was nearly strangling the old man. His eyes were distended as he tried to see the gun pressed against his ear.

"Just get the door open," Savage repeated. He moved toward it, half dragging Alvertone with him. The doctor opened it and Savage went out with the old man, taking the porch steps carefully. The Teepee crew was swarming around the corral, cutting out horses while others straggled from the bunkhouse thirty yards away.

Savage's horse was at the tie rail and he started toward it, trying to avoid the light streaming from the windows and parted door. Alvertone set up a wild struggling and Savage whispered, "Yell, old man, and I'll blow your head off."

Once beside his horse he released Alvertone suddenly and made a downward swipe on the old man's head with his gun barrel. Alvertone dodged and the blow glanced off his shoulder. Without hesitation, Will Savage made the saddle in one leap just as Alvertone began to shout in a loud voice.

"Teepee! Here, Teepee!"

Jabbing spurs to his horse, Savage stormed from the yard. Yells floated up from the vicinity of the corral and a sixgun began a rapid, rolling bleat, trying to search him out.

In a moment he was out of range, riding low against the horse's neck, leaving Alvertone and his wild crew behind.

In the back room of the hotel, Joanne Avery fried a platter of ham and eggs while Owen Frank and young Reilly relaxed at the kitchen table. Gus Avery had retired and the town was quiet now. A large wall clock ticked noisily and when Frank glanced at it he found it to be nearly ten o'clock.

Placing a platter on the table, Joanne laid out butter, warmed-over rolls and two plates, along with the silverware. Taking a chair across from them, she leaned on her folded arms until they finished eating, then rose to get the coffee.

Giving Reilly a close scrutiny, she asked, "What happened to you, Reilly?"

He raised his head abruptly. "Nothing. Why?"

"You think you can go back to Teepee now?"

"I guess not," he said. "I was getting tired of it anyway."

Her eyebrow ascended slightly. "Tired of seventy dollars a month and no work?"

"Maybe," Reilly said defensively, wishing someone would change the subject. He patted his pockets absently and stood up. "Out of tobacco," he mumbled, and took up his hat, leaving hurriedly.

For a moment, Joanne said nothing. Then: "He rolled a cigarette just before he came across the street with you, Owen."

"Let it go," Frank said, and smiled at her. "Reilly's at the fork of the creek. Don't know what's pushing him, but I'd stand back and let him jump if I was you."

Through the door leading into the adjoining room, bed springs protested as Gus Avery stirred fitfully. "We'd better go upstairs," Joanne said. "He's turned into a light sleeper and the slightest noise bothers him."

Cupping her hand around the lamp on the table, she blew it out and stepped into the lobby, closing the door behind her. He followed her up the stairs and walked down the hall with her. Wall lamps washed the hall with yellow light and she opened an unnumbered door.

A touch on his arm halted him while she went in ahead to light three lamps. Stepping inside, he took off his hat, laying it on a table. His hair fell in thick, unruly chunks over his forehead, curling a little behind his ears, and the puffed bruise from Meechum's fist made his angular face slightly lopsided.

Sensing his feeling of awkwardness, Joanne motioned him into a chair. He began to roll a cigarette as she bent to light the fire. She wore a silver gray dress that flowed luxuriously over the slimness of her hips and the pale blue ruffles of her shirtwaist outlined the high collar and sleeves.

Turning quickly, she surprised him in his appraisal and he was unnerved by the amusement in her eyes. "Sorry," he murmured and focussed on his uncompleted cigarette. He finished it and applied a match, drawing deeply on the biting smoke. "I hadn't ought to be here," he said. "There's no reason for it."

"Isn't there?"

He shied away from the answer and hunched down in his chair. Even when he was away from her, her image was clear in his mind: a tall girl with grave eyes and hair the color of spun gold. When he was with her he felt relaxed and full of comfort and he wondered about it. The realization that he was in love with this woman came with disconcerting suddenness. He stiffened his face to keep this new emotion from showing.

Looking around him, he saw the feminine touches that made this a woman's room. Flowered curtains graced the windows and there was a delicate scent of sachet in the air. Swinging his eyes back to her, he found her leaning back against a table, studying him gravely. Her hands were behind her and her hair lay loose and shining over her shoulders.

"I knew you were a troubled man the first moment I saw you," she said. "You're going to stay now, aren't you?"

"Yes," he said, "for a while," and rose to cross to the stove, spinning his cigarette through the damper opening. He stared at the fire through the draft slots, the flames casting dancing patterns on his angular face.

"I was sure of it when you hit Sweikert," Joanne said. "I was glad, Owen, and yet not glad at all. I wanted you to stay because you were tired of riding over hills—but not because you met a challenge and couldn't turn it down."

"A man's what he is," Owen Frank said. "People don't change much."

"I know," she said. "Burk Alvertone won't change. Neither will the farmers. You'll stay until there's no more challenge and then you'll leave." She paused. "Why does it have to be that way, Owen?"

"What's wrong with it?"

"I couldn't live like that—without roots. My life would have to be so that I could look out of the window and see my man working and know he'd come home every night."

Frank spoke gently. "You knew what I was thinking when I was looking at you a moment ago, didn't you?"

"Yes."

"You're not offended?"

"No," she said frankly. "We always measure each other in many ways. A man does it different from a woman because the degree of importance varies." She gave him a wistful smile. "Marrying a man like you might be exciting, Owen—perhaps even dangerous, because there would be no security there, no assurance that tomorrow would dawn in peace. Would it be worth that risk?"

"That's where your values come in," he said, and touched her lightly. She didn't look at him and he slid an arm around her slim shoulders, pulling her gently toward him. She offered no resistance, leaning against him as though it were a welcome relief.

Putting his hand beneath her chin, he tilted her face and then her arms encircled his neck and he was kissing her. He had meant it to be a gentle kiss, soft to show his love and cool to prove that he was not all demanding, but the warm wetness broke through his reserve and he grew rough.

The contradictory expression around her lips that he had noticed was not, he discovered, a product of his imagination, for in the fire of her kiss she offered him a life that was full and complete. It was like diving into a bottomless pool—down without end or the desire for it to end. He released her reluctantly and she touched him on the chest in a final caress before moving near the stove.

Taking out his tobacco again, he found that his hands shook when he tried to form a cigarette. Finally he said, "That wasn't very wise, was it?"

"Not very," she agreed in an unsteady voice. "We'd

never make a go of it, Owen. We're fools to even think of it."

"Fools live short, happy lives," he murmured, and studied the pointed ash on his cigarette. "You wouldn't like that?"

"My roots have to be down deep," she said. "I want my house built on rock."

"Like those farmers?"

"Not like them," she said, "but wanting what they want." She turned around and took his arm. "I guess we both want something we can't have."

"We can have it," he told her, "but would we be satisfied afterward? One of these days I'll leave and you'll forget all about me. You'll marry Will Savage and be happy. That's the way life goes."

"Does it?" She laughed shortly and moved over to the window, parting the curtains to look down at the street. "We're lying, Owen. Neither one of us is going to forget. Maybe you'll find a woman for you—one who'll be content to move when the weather changes. You'll be happy but I'll hate her for making you happy when I couldn't."

Owen Frank picked up his hat and walked to the door. He hesitated, but she didn't turn around. "Good night, Joanne."

"Good night," she said, and she was still looking out of the window when he closed the door and went down the hall to his own room.

Someone had repaired the door and he went inside, lighting the lamp. His bed was propped up again and the broken furniture placed in a corner. Sitting on the edge of the bed, he removed his boots and socks, then stripped off his coat and shirt. He poured water into the bowl, washed to the waist and blew out the lamp.

He hung his gun over the corner post of the bed and removed his pants, settling down for the night. Lying on his side made the bruises on his face ache so he rolled over on his back, lacing his hands beneath his head.

The memory of Joanne's lips was strong and he could still feel the supple length of her strained against him. What she had offered him she had never offered before to any other man, and yet it had not been enough to quench his restlessness.

Accepting would have been easy, for he was young and

time was still relative to him, a month or a year making little difference. But when he grew older? Would he regret the things he could have seen and done? She deserved better than that.

Some day along the trail he would grow weary of this life and stop. He was positive of that. But right now he had to keep moving. A man couldn't help the way he felt about things. He had to take life as it was offered and be happy with it.

Only he wasn't happy and he knew it.

The thought kept him awake for better than an hour and then he fell asleep.

A sharp rapping on his door caused him to sit bolt upright. His watch showed the time to be near midnight. The pounding grew more insistent and he pulled on his pants hurriedly. "I'm coming," he said.

When he opened the door Joanne Avery placed her hands against his bare chest and pushed him back. "Owen, Will Savage just came into town. He says Alvertone's crew is right behind him. They're going to sack the grove!"

Frank cursed and began to put on his shirt. "Light a lamp," he said, and sat down to tug on his boots. "Where's Reilly?"

"I don't know. He didn't come back. Owen, you've got to stop them!"

"That's Will Savage's job," he said. "He ran for sheriff, I didn't."

"He can't hold them alone," she cried, kneading her hands. "He's waiting for you downstairs."

"The damn fool," Frank said, and buckled on his gunbelt. He went out without hat or coat, hurrying down the stairs. Savage was waiting in the lobby, pacing up and down like a nervous animal.

"Frank," Savage said, "I—"

"Let's get the hell over there," Frank said, and was out the door before Savage got into motion. The sheriff looked at Joanne, poised at the head of the stairs, her wooly robe drawn tight about her. He meant to speak, then waved his hands in a futile gesture and ran after Frank.

The street was dark at this hour, only a few night lamps in the shops casting a dim light on the boardwalk as they ran toward the bridge. There was no sound at all in the sleeping town other than the pound of their boots on the wooden walk.

As they neared the bridge, Frank slowed for Savage to catch up with him. "How far behind?"

"Fifteen minutes—who knows?"

They crossed the bridge and took the rutted wagon road leading to the grove, stumbling in the darkness. A hushed gloom lay over the wagon camp, for the fires had died down to glowing coals. As they approached, Frank drew his gun and fired twice into the air. Immediately he was answered by frightened calls from the various wagons.

"Build up your fires!" Frank called. He veered toward a man who jumped down, dressed in a long, flannel nightshirt and waving a double barreled shotgun.

"Don't come any closer!" the man shouted, and pointed the gun.

"You damn fool—Alvertone's sending a bunch to raid you!"

Frank's yell set the camp alive.

Savage began to heap brush on a fire and as the feeble flame took hold and grew, it threw out an ever widening circle of light. Other men began to rebuild their fires and soon it was possible to see across the compound.

They were none too quick. Out on the flats they could hear the growing thunder of running horses.

Savage was dashing back and forth, shouting orders and getting the men into position to defend the grove. As Owen Frank watched them he realized suddenly that if anyone started shooting, the farmers would be beaten with the first trigger pull. All the cowboys wore guns and they knew how to use them.

Cupping his hands around his mouth, he shouted, "Savage, listen to me—no guns! Get me a stout rope and find yourselves some hoe and pick handles—but no shooting!"

For a stupefied moment, the men gaped at Frank, then moved into action. One long legged farmer came up with a large coil of thick rope. Frank tied one end to the axle of a heavy farm wagon. Taking the coil, he unrolled it as he ran across the mouth of the camp. He secured it to the rear wheel of an old ore wagon, drawing it knee high and tight as he could pull it.

Savage joined Frank, worry plain on his clean features. "Dammit," he said. "Why do you say no guns?"

The pound of the Teepee riders was growing alarmingly close.

"Start shooting," Frank said, "and there'll be a lot of dead men tonight. A cowboy is plenty proud and getting the hell whacked out of him with a hoe handle will dent his pride a lot easier than a bullet. Now get the men around these end wagons and the women and children at the other end of the grove in those trees."

There was no need for Savage to give the order. Several farmers had already clutched the idea and the camp was soon vacated. The running horses were less than a half mile away now and there were only a few minutes left.

Frank split his forces, the men all armed with pick handles and chunks of heavy wood. Fifteen crouched behind the wagon, while another dozen took cover in the brush by the mouth of the grove.

On came the Teepee crew, yelling now. Their blood was hot and they were ready for a night's fun. The rope strung across the opening was almost invisible in the firelight.

"Get set," Frank said.

The riders stormed off the road, taking the lane leading into the farmers' camp. They rode fast and proud without heed for danger, smugly confident of their superiority, and when the first wave struck the rope, eight abreast, the force was enough to topple both wagons with a side-splitting crash.

A dozen of Alvertone's men were spilled in the first rush and the ones following immediately behind became hopelessly tangled among the downed and screaming horses.

A veritable bedlam arose as the farmers darted from their places of concealment, handles swinging, whooping like Indians. The farmers had the complete advantage for the moment as the few men who remained mounted backed off uncertainly.

The cursing and yelling rose in a sheet of sound and one Teepee hand went down with a stick laid across his skull. Another man, still mounted, pulled his gun and leveled it but a farmer swung an ax handle in a vicious arc and fractured the rider's arm with one blow.

Teepee was not winning this and they knew it. Most of the downed horses were now on their feet again and running free of the melee, while the battle raged thick and fast behind them. Half the Teepee crew was down and

64

out in the first minute, while from the others, still mounted and wheeling away, came the first burst of shooting.

A farmer reeled from the fight with a bullet-shattered arm and Frank whirled, spotting the rider getting ready to shoot again. Closing the distance in two jumps, Frank clubbed him across the back of the neck with his gun and watched him wilt.

A half dozen Teepee hands still remained on their horses but had withdrawn away from the camp. Some of the farmers were eager to follow but Frank yelled, "Let them go! Let them go!"

Savage ran over to Frank and said, "We've got 'em on the run. Now let's keep 'em that way."

"Be better to rub it in a little," Frank said, and made a megaphone of his hands. "Teepee? Rankin, can you hear me?"

"I hear you," Rankin called from the darkness.

"Come in and get your friends," Frank yelled. "No guns now or you'll get hurt!"

For a moment of dead silence, it looked as if there wouldn't be an answer. But at last Rankin called back, "How about sendin' 'em out?"

"Come on in if you want 'em. Can't you stand to take a licking?"

An angry growl went up from the Teepee men at this. Frank turned to the farmers. "Disarm them and get them in one bunch. The ones that can't walk can be carried."

There was the soft sound of hooves in the dust on the road and the remaining Teepee riders, led by Rankin, moved forward cautiously. The firelight touched them and Frank said, "Dismount and help 'em out of here."

"You'll get yours for this," Rankin said bitterly.

"Don't push your luck, friend," Owen advised. "You've just taken the licking of your life and if you want some more, just sing out."

They got down and began to help their friends. Some of the downed men were coming around. A few could stand, but there were plenty of sore heads.

"What about their horses?" Rankin asked.

"They can walk home," Frank said, and smiled at the shock that appeared on the man's face. He understood how far it was and he well knew how tortuous high heeled boots could be for walking. "Maybe you'll all remember this better if you have a few blisters. Get going now and you can make it by daylight."

"Be a sonovabitch if I will!" one man said flatly.

"Knock him down," Owen said in an emotionless tone, and a farmer obliged, flattening the rider with one sweep of a hoe handle.

This brought a dull murmar from the Teepee men. Frank said, "This little party can get mighty rough, boys. What'll it be—walk away from it or fight some more?"

"You're a dead man, Frank," Rankin said. "You don't know it yet, that's all."

"Get 'em out of here," Frank said, and the farmers began to crowd forward, driving the cowboys out of the camp with their clubs. Savage and Frank stood by one of the overturned wagons and when Savage tried to light a cigar, he found that his hands trembled.

"That was close," he said. "Damn close."

"A lot of fights are," Owen Frank said dryly. The women began to leave the protection of the trees to join the men. Some of the farmers had been injured, how badly Frank didn't know. He sighed, knowing that was part of the price they had to pay for being here.

Feeling out of place among the farmers now that he was no longer needed, he headed out of the grove and walked slowly back to Painted Rock.

CHAPTER 6

After an early breakfast in the restaurant, Owen Frank walked to the jail and rapped on the heavy door. He heard an answering grumble from Savage and went in.

The sheriff had a mirror propped up on his desk and was shaving carefully. He looked at Frank, motioned toward a chair and went on with his work. Finally he toweled his face dry and put the shaving gear in the bottom drawer.

"Quite a night, wasn't it?"

"Not too good for Teepee," Frank said, and shook out

the makings. He crossed his long legs and built his smoke, saying nothing more until he had it going. "What are you going to do about this?"

"Keep a lot of people from getting killed, if I can."

"Teepee or the farmers?"

"What do you mean by that?" Savage snapped. He waved his hand absently and walked over to the window, looking out on the vacant street. A sharp wind whipped down between the double row of buildings, whirling dust along before it. "I know what you mean," he said heavily. "I'm on neither side. Understand that."

"It won't work," Frank said. "You'll have to get off the fence. You're either for Alvertone or you're against him. Which is it?"

"Neither, dammit!" Savage took a cigar from his pocket, scissored off the end with his teeth and touched a match to it. "Frank, I'm not like you. I'd rather arbitrate—come to a sensible conclusion—than push Burk Alvertone off his place."

"How far do you think you'd have got last night with talk?" Owen pointed out.

"Agh," Savage said. "I was out to Teepee. Alvertone was hot because you roughed him and Sweikert up. He wanted to get even by raiding the grove."

"Regardless of the reason," Frank said, "men could have been killed. You'd have had a full scale war on your hands then, man. You may still have it, if those farmers decide to break camp and squat on Teepee grass."

After pulling thoughtfully on his cigar for a moment, Savage shied it into the spittoon and sat down at his desk, his handsome face worried. "I'm not denying this, Frank— I'm a cattleman sheriff. Alvertone's influence got me elected and his influence will shove me out. For eighteen years, Teepee money has kept this town going. You can see why I have to listen when Burk Alvertone talks."

"You're playing a fool's game," Owen said. "Do you think these farmers are the last who are going to come here?" He laughed. "In ten more years this land will be cut up with fences and small farms. If there's any cattle left, it'll be on a smaller scale and then Alvertone won't be supporting Painted Rock. Which side are you going to be on, Will Savage—the winners' or the losers'?"

Leaning forward on his desk, Savage pawed his face out of shape. Finally he said, "Your way and mine are different, Frank. I'm trying to avoid a fight."

"You think I'm not?"

Savage slapped the desk. "I don't know, Frank. I really don't. You killed Showers and now you've stirred up Alvertone and Sweikert. Reilly's out of it for some reason. He stayed in town last night, sleeping in the stable loft. Last night you made a life enemy of Rankin, and he's not the forgiving kind either." Savage leaned forward and studied Owen Frank carefully. "What are you trying to do? What's in this for you? I didn't ask you for your help."

"Are you turning it down?"

"Yes," Savage said. "No hard feelings, Frank, but this is my responsibility. I can handle it alone, my way. Yours is no good."

"That's putting it plain enough," Frank said, and stood up. He gave Savage a worried glance and went out.

A brisk wind had come up, fresh and biting, out of the northwest, and clouds covered the sky like a canopy with little break in their rolled surface. The daylight was gray and dismal and Buffalo Street was nearly denuded of traffic as Owen Frank paced the length of it.

Crossing the wooden bridge, he followed the wagon road leading into the grove. Cookfires still burned high and there was considerable activity. The two wagons that had been overturned the night before had been righted and now sat with canvas sagging over their fractured bows. One man had set up a blacksmith shop and was repairing a wheel rim while a half grown boy pumped the bellows.

Spotting Fred Meechum's wagon, Owen crossed the compound to where the man squatted before his fire. Lottie and her mother were busy with a washing and after casual nods they ignored Frank.

Meechum's face was not so swollen this morning and he seemed in better spirits. He said, "Where the hell did you run off to last night, man? I'm thinking we all owe you thanks."

"You don't owe me anything," Frank said. "Killing is senseless."

"To that I'll agree," Meechum said, and lifted a burning stick to light his pipe.

"How many got hurt?" Frank asked.

"Five. Murdock is laid up with a busted arm. Somebody shot him and broke the bone. The others are just bumps." He chuckled. "I never saw such a whipped bunch as that Teepee outfit."

"They're not whipped," Frank told him. "Meechum, there's an election coming up and Teepee is going to win it. This country won't be healthy for a man with a plow when that happens."

"We're voting for Savage," Meechum said flatly. "We have enough here to swing it with the tradesmen's help."

"They'll vote Teepee. That's where the money is right now."

"Oh hell," Meechum said. He fell silent, a great worry in his eyes.

Glancing around, Owen Frank noticed a wide gap between two parked wagons. This puzzled him, for last night all the wagons had been drawn close together. "What happened to those two wagons over there?" he asked Meechum.

"Pulled out last night," Meechum said.

"Leaving the country?"

"No. They moved onto Teepee grass."

For a moment, Owen Frank said nothing. He understood how it was with a man, taking all he could and then some more. The first victory was always the most exhilarating, the most overwhelming. False hope was easy to cling to and these men had invited disaster by moving onto Burk Alvertone's range.

"Better send someone out there after them," he warned. "They might be buying into something too big for them to carry."

"Hyslip and Oldfield know what they're doing," Meechum said. "They're stubborn men and once their minds is set on something, all hell couldn't shake 'em loose."

"How many went?"

"Hyslip and his son. Oldfield was alone. His wife and daughter died on the way across."

Rising from his haunches, Owen said, "You feel like stumpin' for the sheriff this morning?"

Meechum looked a little surprised but said, "If you think it'll do any good." He rose and took his coat and

69

hat from the back of the wagon. His wife still bent over her wooden tub and he called to her, "Emma, I'm going uptown."

"Stay out of the saloons," she said without turning her head, and Meechum walked away with Owen Frank.

Passing through the camp, Frank returned a dozen friendly nods. Meechum saw this and said, "You made a big impression last night."

"They won the fight," Frank said curtly. "I didn't."

Reaching Buffalo Street, Owen turned into the mercantile, Fred Meechum following. The owner was busy sweeping down the floor but he paused when Owen Frank and the big farmer leaned against the counter.

"What can I do for you gentlemen?"

"We'd like to talk about politics," Frank told him, and watched the wariness cross the man's face. He was a typical tradesman, slightly built with a rotund stomach. The man went behind the counter and began to dust.

"I take little interest in politics," he said diffidently.

"Now is the time to take a big interest," Frank assured him. "We'd like to see Will Savage stay on as the sheriff." The man continued to dust and Frank reached across the counter, taking the feather duster out of his hand. "Don't act so busy, friend. What we're talking about is your future in Painted Rock."

"My future's secure," the man said shortly. "Now, if you'll excuse me, I have a lot to do." He tried to take the duster back but Frank pulled it out of his reach. "Now, see here—" he began testily, but caught the glint in Frank's eyes and fell silent.

"Let me tell you a little story," Frank said, seating himself on the counter. "When you started in business here you had quite a few ranches to trade with, but as time passed you lost your customers while one man got bigger and bigger. Now Burk Alvertone is your only customer and his crew keeps you going. Who's making money here? You, or Alvertone? One of these days you're going to have a hassle with one of the Teepee crew and they'll take you apart. Who are you going to turn to then? The sheriff? Alvertone will own him. Alvertone himself? He'll laugh at you. And if you get tough he'll run you out and put someone else in here. How do you like that story, mister?"

"Granting what you say is true," the man said, "I still see no solution."

"Here's your solution," Frank said, and nodded toward Meechum. "Men like him who don't carry a gun. They buy more than ropes and saddles, mister. They buy plows and wagons and tools. They're the men Will Savage is backing. You'd better vote carefully this time or maybe Alvertone will do away with elections once he gets the law under his thumb."

"I—I'm just a little man. What can I do by myself?"

"You're not going to be alone," Frank said. "If Will Savage loses this election, there won't be much left of Painted Rock in another ten years. The country's going to grow, friend. Railroads will come, and more farmers. But they won't come here now because Alvertone won't let them. All around you there's going to be prosperity, but you won't be in on it because the same old crowd will be ramrodding the show."

Nodding to Fred Meechum, Frank walked out with the big farmer trailing along behind. For an hour they went from one establishment to another before crossing the street to the saloon.

Felix was behind the bar. Owen Frank spun a dollar on the polished cherrywood. "The good bottle," he said, and leaned heavily.

The bartender poured and handed Frank his change. "How's business?" Frank asked.

"Never changes," Felix admitted. "One week a month I'm rich. The other days it hardly pays me to stay open."

"Would you rather sell whisky for five days or beer all month long?"

"How's that again?"

Frank leaned forward and spoke confidentially. "At the coming election, you're going to have a choice between the farmers' trade and Burk Alvertone's. Now a farmer doesn't carry a gun and shoot holes in your ceiling. He drinks a few beers, plays a hand or two of poker and goes about his business. The nice thing about it, Felix, is that it's steady business. A business that will grow when more farmers come in."

"I've thought about it," Felix admitted, and moved the bar rag listlessly. "You think Savage is going to beat Sweikert?"

"If he gets the town vote, he will," Frank said. "You know as well as I do that Alvertone owns Painted Rock. He's going to start putting the squeeze on the merchants by next week. Vote his way or no more trade. You get it?"

"I get it," Felix agreed. "I don't like it either."

"He's going to make you like it," Frank said. "How's it going to be, Felix?"

The man gnawed his lip for a moment and then threw down his bar rag, nodding toward the back room. Opening a door, he stepped aside and they filed into his small office. Once seated, he got to the point.

"Frank, if I was for Alvertone, you'd never have taken him out that door the other night. Under the bar there's a double-barreled shotgun and I'd have used it." He glanced at Fred Meechum. "I, for one, want the farmers here. They're not as wild and they make a country grow. But I'll tell you this right now—you'll never beat Alvertone's game by going around to the merchants like this."

"You tell me a better way," Frank invited.

"All right. Idaho's a territory," Felix said. "We don't have a legitimate county, but we've set it up as if we had. There's four men in this town that make up the county board. I'm one of them. Gus Avery's another. Jules Blankenship at the feedstore is the third, and Hy Linnet, the Wells Fargo agent, is the fourth. Does that give you any ideas?"

"It does," Frank said. "You four set the election dates?"

"That's one of our duties," Felix admitted. He studied Owen Frank carefully.

"How hard would it be to get these men together?"

"Not hard at all," Felix said. "You and Meechum go on over to the hotel. I'll get Blankenship and Linnet and meet you there in a few minutes."

Frank grinned and stood up. "Felix, I like you."

"I like a fighter," the saloon keeper said. "Personally, I'm too damned old and fat now, but that don't mean I can't pass the ammunition."

"Thanks," Frank said, and went out with Meechum. Crossing the street, they made for the hotel, heads down against the driving wind. Clouds of stinging dust rose from the street, and in the alley a loose window shutter pivoted on a hinge, banging away at the wall.

Entering the lobby, Frank found Joanne Avery behind the desk. He said, "Is your father up?"

She nodded. "He just finished breakfast."

"We're going to have a board meeting," he said. "Felix and the others are coming over."

"Is there something wrong?"

He smiled. "This time I hope something's right." He took her hand and she came with him. Rapping on the door, he heard Gus Avery's answering voice and went in.

"Well," the old man said, and tried to hide his cigar from his daughter. "I hear Teepee went home with their tails between their legs last night."

"There were some bruises," Frank admitted.

Joanne walked around behind her father's chair, took the cigar away from him and threw it into the stove. "Dammit," he said.

Meechum took a chair, sitting uncomfortably on the edge, and a moment later another knock sounded. Joanne crossed the room to let in Felix, Blankenship and Linnet.

Jules Blankenship was a tall man, stringy, with a sad face that reminded Frank somewhat of a beagle hound. He had bony wrists and long fingers with dark hair curling thickly on the backs. Linnet was a small man with quick, dark eyes and a driving manner.

Felix said, "You got the floor, Frank."

Because he knew none of these men well, nor where their sympathies lay, he chose his words carefully. Easing into the subject, he explained how the economic future of Painted Rock depended on the influx of farmers and not one man. He conceded that if there had been a dozen ranches in the district, he would be against a farmer-cowman war; but the only ranch here was Teepee.

By pointing up the dangers of a one-man empire, he held their attention. Then he broached his plan to defeat Alvertone in the coming election.

"Gentlemen," he said, "I would like to see the election date moved up to tomorrow or the day after, at the latest."

This set them all talking at once, and for a minute the room buzzed. Then Gus Avery beat on the floor with his cane, bringing quiet.

"I've listened and I like the sound of it," he said. "I guess we all know Burk and what he's fighting for, but it all boils down to these facts. One: the land ain't his—it belongs to the government and it's open for settlement. Two: on election day, Teepee is going to take over Painted Rock. He's too smart a man to tell another how to vote, but if he wants to get rough, his men will keep the farmers away from the polls. Three: there's the question of which is more honest, Owen Frank's way, or Burk Alvertone's. I vote to move the election up to tomorrow and have notices printed to that effect."

"I'll second that," Felix said.

Hy Linnet pulled at his lip for a moment. "I don't own property in Painted Rock and Wells Fargo pays me a steady wage, but I know what Frank says is so. The town will never grow with one man at the reins. I'll cast my vote with Gus and Felix."

"I can't do it," Jules Blankenship stated flatly. "I'm in the feed business. Without Alvertone's money, I'm as good as dead. Sorry, but that's the way it is."

"You're already dead then," Frank said. "The vote's three to one against you and Alvertone won't stop to ask which way you voted. He'll crawl down your throat and make a nest."

Blankenship looked worriedly at the others. "The position you place me in is hardly fair," he said.

"That proves my point," Frank said. "If you ever doubted how large was Alvertone's control, now you know. Even you gentlemen are in some way swayed and you're supposed to be impartial."

"I never looked at it that way," Blankenship said. "By thunder, I'll change my vote. He's been complaining about the price of feed—let him get it someplace else. I'll do my business with the farmers from now on."

"We'll consider the issue settled then," Gus Avery said. "Felix, see that Will Savage is notified and have handbills printed for immediate distribution."

The saloon keeper smiled at Frank and went out. Blankenship glanced at Linnet, then back to Frank. There was a new admiration in the tall man's eyes. "The other night I mistook you for one of Sweikert's stripe. That was my mistake." He touched Linnet on the arm and they left.

Gus Avery said, "Wish to hell you hadn't thrown my cigar away, girl."

"I'll get you another one," Joanne said, and crossed to the bureau. She peeled the band from a Moonshine Crook and scratched a match for him. The old man puffed for a moment in deep contentment, then settled back in his chair.

"You haven't won the election yet," he said, drawing easily on his cigar. "Joanne, honey, fix your old dad a cup of coffee."

"This isn't your birthday," she told him scoldingly, but filled the pot and set it on the stove. Turning her head, she gazed for a long moment at Owen Frank until she caught Meechum watching her. She grew slightly flustered then and turned her back to them.

"And if you do win the election," Gus went on, "where does that leave you? The farmers will still be camped at the grove and Alvertone will be holding all that land under his thumb." Gus Avery shook his head. "Ah, Frank, you're smart and you're tough, but I'm wondering if that's enough."

Sitting with his head down, he nursed his cigar until Joanne handed him a half cup of coffee.

Swan Oldfield was no longer a young man but a lifetime of habit pushed at him, driving him onward when he no longer really wanted to move. All of his life had been one prolonged labor to produce from the soil, and with his wife and daughter beside him he had found contentment in the task. But now he was alone, his family buried on a small knoll by the north fork of the Platte, and the old purpose to life was gone. He wanted only to sit in the sun and watch the world go by.

A few yards ahead, Lige Hyslip and his lanky son sat their wagon, moving deeper into grass that grew cannon-deep. The wind slashed across the valley, carrying with it the promise of weather. The canvas tops whipped before the force of it, popping and snapping against the bows.

By noon, they were ready to angle north toward the creek that split this rich valley. Hyslip and his son built a small fire, inviting Swan Oldfield to join them at their frugal meal.

After Hyslip had cleaned his plate of beans, he pointed with his fork. "Yonder's a place. I heard a cattleman owned it once but Alvertone drove him out. We'll take that. We need shelter with weather in the making."

Once the fire was stamped out, the wagons creaked

northward and an hour later Hyslip sighted the remains of the abandoned ranch. The cabin was still intact, a two-room affair with a burned-out barn and corral to the north. As they approached, Hyslip studied the barn. It told a complete story. The fire had been started on the inside, for the rafters had burned through first, allowing the walls to cave in against each other, forming a crude pyramid. Evidently a rain had come up in time to extinguish it, for the walls were charred near the top but still sound at the bottom.

The corral was nothing more than a few vertical posts and sagging, burned-through cross bars. As they drew nearer, Hyslip's son touched his father's arm and pointed to the east. On a slight rise, two riders remained poised and motionless for a long moment, then wheeled and disappeared from sight.

The old man's face showed a grave concern, but he made no comment.

A long stack of bucked wood nestled against the east wall of the cabin, and behind this sat two outbuildings, one a large tack shed and the other a slant-roofed stall with a large quarter moon sawed into the leather-hung door.

Dismounting by what remained of the barn, Hyslip turned the team over to his son, and with Oldfield's help, began to carry their supplies into the cabin.

On the third trip, Oldfield paused to mop sweat from his brow. He said, "Did you see them? There's trouble here."

"Nothing's free," Hyslip said shortly, and lifted a heavy box.

By early evening they had the cabin cleaned out, the provisions stored and a fire roaring in the stove. Outside, the wind picked up, moaning loudly around the corners of the building. The three men huddled around the fire, saying little, each preferring his own solitary thoughts.

The first of the Teepee crew arrived at Alvertone's ranch after the breakfast triangle had clanged and he waited on his wide porch, an old man plagued by a deep-rooted worry. Across the flats he saw them coming in a staggered string. Half a dozen men were mounted but staying loyally with their less fortunate friends.

It took them an hour to walk the last stretch and only

one man came to the porch where Alvertone waited. The others limped to the bunkhouse and disappeared inside.

A temper flamed in the old man's eyes and he lashed out in a harsh voice, "You damn infants! What the hell happened?"

"We got licked," Rankin said. He looked disgusted. On his face there was a deep stain of fatigue and a dried streak of blood traced its way from the caked split in his scalp.

"Rankin, are you a foreman or a snot-nosed kid?"

"I'm a foreman," Rankin said. "They was waitin' for us, Burk. We didn't have a chance."

"Didn't have a chance?" The old man's eyes blazed. "Dammit, you had guns! What more do you need?"

"Frank was there," Rankin said sourly. "He had a rope stretched between two wagons and we hit it full tilt. The sodbusters was waitin' and lit into us with pick handles." Rankin sat down on the steps, pillowing his head in his hands. "We got licked, but we didn't get licked no worse than that gun dummy you got in there." He nodded his head toward the bunkhouse where Sweikert lay.

"Licked you," Alvertone said as though he couldn't believe it. "You let those farmers run you off like a bunch of cur dogs." He doubled his fist and raised it as if he were going to hit Rankin. Finally he dropped it to his side and wheeled into the house, slamming the door after him.

Throughout the morning and early afternoon, Alvertone stayed to himself, smoking one cigar after another and pacing up and down his wide living room. Like most men who battle for power and achieve it, he was learning how much greater and more continuous was the battle to keep it.

The defeat at the grove rankled, but it was a surface anger. His main rage was directed at Owen Frank. From the beginning Alvertone had read danger in the man.

He was standing by his window when two of his line riders rode into the yard, dismounted by the porch and strode purposefully into the house without invitation. It was on his mind to call them for this, but one look at their faces made him forget about it.

A red-headed puncher whisked off his hat and said, "Boss, there's two wagons at the old Grover place. Me and Ace here watched 'em."

"From the grove?"

"Where else?" Ace asked.

"All right." Alvertone rotated his cigar. "Send Rankin in here right away."

"Sure," Ace said, and the two men went out and across the yard. Standing by the front window, Alvertone watched them enter the bunkhouse. A moment later, Rankin appeared, walking rapidly across the dusty yard.

The wind had picked up and Rankin walked on a list against it, one hand raised to secure his wide-brimmed hat. He stomped across the porch and came in.

"Did Ace tell you?" Alvertone asked.

"He told me." In Rankin's eyes there was a naked eagerness.

"Take Ace, Shaw and Buck along with you and burn them out tonight," Alvertone said flatly. "If those sodbusters are allowed to stay, there'll be no stopping the others. Do a good job out there, you understand?"

"I understand." Rankin moved toward the door, pausing as though halted by an afterthought. "About Sweikert— it'd be just as well to pay him off. He's no good to us now."

"I'll do the hirin' and firin' around here," Alvertone told him. "You get on about your business."

Shrugging his shoulders, Rankin went out, slamming the door behind him. Alvertone stayed near the window, watching his foreman gather his crew and cross to the corral for horses. He didn't understand Miles Rankin and this worried him, for Alvertone took pride in the way he read men. For months now, Rankin had been on the peck about something and no amount of talk wormed it out of him.

Five minutes later Rankin and his crew rode from the yard. Burk Alvertone turned away from the window, worried and not understanding the source.

CHAPTER 7

The wind whistling through the cracks in the siding woke Reilly late in the morning. He shook himself free from his

78

burrow of straw and went down the ladder to the stable floor.

Through the long night he had turned many things over in his mind, and he had decided to get out now, before he made a foolish mistake. His horse was in a back stall. He saddled up, then led the animal to the back door and mounted.

Riding through the thickets behind the town, Reilly angled toward the river. He intended to cross to the grove, but decided against it. He wouldn't dare speak to her in plain sight of the farmers, and since he was known as Alvertone's man, he was sure that it would be unsafe to make an appearance in any capacity.

Now he was free to follow his own whims and solitary fancies and yet this did not leave him with the feeling of relief that he had anticipated.

Traveling in a wide circle, Reilly found himself southwest of town, headed toward the open badlands and lava beds. The wind out here reached gale proportions and he rode hunched over in the saddle, his back twisted to shield him somewhat.

A more desolate country he had never seen. He had thought so when he and Sweikert first traversed it months before. It seemed more like years now.

Maybe he should have gone to the grove and taken her with him; but he realized that a woman had to want to be with her man and he had no assurance that Lottic Meechum liked him enough.

By mid-afternoon he was in the midst of the lava beds, an eerie land that plagued him with a crawling sensation. The spatter cones and deep fissures lent an alien unreality to the land that made the horse skittish and Reilly nervous. The wind moaned around these weird formations, creating new tones on nature's organ.

Squatting down near the protection of a lava cone, Reilly pondered his decision to run. Finally, when his conscience grew bothersome, he remounted and began to retrace his path back to Painted Rock.

Entering town again as night began to fall, Reilly took his horse back to the stable, grained him, and walked over the bridge to the grove. Cookfires were being built high against the growing darkness and he skirted the wagon park to work his way through the shrubs and timber encircling the grove.

He made his way unerringly to the Meechum wagon and hunkered down where he could view the activity nearby. Lottie and her mother were preparing the evening meal. Reilly waited until Lottie came around the back of the wagon. Then tossed a small pebble that struck the hem of her dress, causing her to give a frightened start.

Her mother raised her head. "Land's sake, girl, what's the matter with you?"

"Nothing," Lottie said quickly. "I thought I saw a snake."

"No snakes around here," her mother scoffed. "Hurry up with that breadboard."

"All right." Lottie peered into the brush but saw nothing. She lifted her skirts and climbed into the wagon, groping around in the thick darkness until she found the board. She knew she should take it to her mother, but still she hesitated. Finally she heard a faint scraping against the canvas and lifted the bottom edge slightly.

"I'll be waiting," Reilly whispered.

"I can't. Not again."

"I'll be waiting," he repeated, and disappeared.

"Land's sakes," her mother called. "Haven't you found that breadboard yet?"

"I'm coming." Lottie jumped down, hoping desperately that nothing showed on her face. Her mother gave her a sharp appraisal as she took the board. Even her father raised his head to study her for what seemed a long time.

"What's the matter with you?" her mother asked. "First you think you seen a snake and now you're acting jumpy as a cat."

"Nothing," Lottie insisted, and lowered her head. Her cheeks felt aflame.

"I don't know what's got into the child," her mother complained in a droning voice. "I do wish you'd find her a man, Fred. She'd ought to be married at her age. Wish we'd stayed in Illinois. We had a good place there."

"We'll have a good place here," Fred Meechum said solidly. "You worry too much, woman."

"Hah," she said. "What's land if my man's dead? Coming home with your face so beat a body can't recognize you. I hate this place!"

"Good land," Meechum maintained stubbornly. "Mighty fine land."

"I—I think I'll take a walk," Lottie said.

"Land's sakes, supper'll be ready in a half hour. Can't you wait?"

"I won't be long, Ma," Lottie said, and hurried away from the fire.

"What's possessed that girl?" the older woman muttered.

"I don't know." Meechum packed his pipe slowly, staring all the while into the darker shadows along the fringe of the camp.

Once away from her parents' eyes, Lottie quickly changed direction and angled toward the river. She moved slowly, for the night tricked her and the brush snagged her dress. She reached the bank and dropped down to the soft, narrow beach between bank and water, moving more swiftly now until she saw a man's shadow rise just ahead of her.

Reilly said, "I just had to see you, Lottie."

"I can't come here any more," she said. "My folks can always tell when I'm lying, Reilly. I can't do it no more."

"Then *don't* lie no more," he said. "Lottie, we got to come out in the open with this."

"With—with what?" she asked tremulously.

For a moment he faltered, wondering if she cared enough for him. "I—I thought we liked each other, Lottie."

"Yes, yes," she said. "But Pa would never let you come near this place. Don't come any more, Reilly. He has funny ideas about fellas."

"Is that what you want—me not to come around?"

"No," she said. "It isn't, but we don't want trouble."

"We didn't start this mess," Reilly protested. "Lottie, it isn't our fault that Alvertone and your pa are on opposite sides. I've broke with Teepee, Lottie. Can't they see that?"

"They don't want to see it, Reilly. Please, now—I have to get back."

"Wait! I left Painted Rock this morning, intending to stay away. But I had to come back. Don't you understand why, Lottie?"

"I understand," she whispered, and touched him gently. "Some day there'll be a time and place for us, but not now. I'm as sorry as you are."

"I reckon I love you," Reilly murmured. "Funny how it happened, ain't it?"

"It just happened," she said. "It just—honest, Reilly, I have to go—"

She took two steps up the bank and bumped into her father's legs.

Involuntarily she cried out in alarm. Reilly saw only the looming shadow of a man. He took the bank at a plunging run. Meechum raised a knee and slammed Reilly in the chest, kicking him backward into the creek.

Lottie screamed. The bobbing glow of lanterns flickered through the trees as men came forward on the run.

Reilly floundered in water that was waist deep, his chest a solid ache where Meechum's knee had caught him. The big man jumped down the bank as Reilly waded toward shore. Reilly threw a blind punch and connected, but he was off balance and the blow lacked power.

Encircling the young man with his arms, Meechum applied his tremendous strength. Reilly cried out as his ribs threatened to crack. A dozen men lined the bank now, their lanterns shooting glistening light on the river as the two men struggled.

"A couple of you fellas give me a hand with this jasper," Meechum said, and two men slithered down, seizing Reilly roughly and dragging him up the bank. Lottie was crying and begging them not to hurt him but her father slapped her across the mouth.

"Get back to the wagon," he thundered. "I'll tend to you later."

She ran on ahead of the men, stumbling and weeping, while Reilly was forced, fighting and kicking, to the center of the grove. Men and women crowded around to see this and children dodged and ducked, trying to work their way through the forest of legs that formed a ring around Reilly and Meechum.

They stood by a large fire and dancing shadows flickered redly over their faces. Reilly stood spraddle-legged, water dripping in a muddy puddle between his feet.

One man moved in behind him and took his gun as he

stepped back. Meechum said, "You low scum, I'm going to change your face so a mother couldn't love it."

Lottie screamed "No!" and tried to get to him, but her mother slapped her soundly and finally pinned her against the wagon with her bulk. Lottie's wild crying filled the camp, overriding the mutter of men's voices.

"Fool with a decent girl, will you!" Meechum said, and shuffled forward, his fists cocked, his heavy boots shuffling in the dust. He charged the last five feet, swinging heavily. Reilly ducked and danced back.

A bearded man at the edge of the crowd stepped forward and hit the young man at the base of the skull, driving him forward and into Meechum's axing fist.

Men groaned in spite of themselves at the sodden impact and Reilly cartwheeled backward to roll over and brace himself painfully on his hands and knees. His open mouth was bleeding profusely and on the ground between his hands were two teeth.

Meechum seized the young man by the hair, jerking him upright with his bull strength. Reilly made a pawing motion at the big man but Meechum ignored it. He struck Reilly in the stomach, bringing his mouth open, windless and in constricted agony.

Methodically then, Meechum pounded Reilly's face to shapelessness. Both eyes were puffed closed and the young man's nose was askew when Meechum released him, allowing him to drop. For Reilly there was no remembrance of the last dozen blows. Consciousness had left him.

Bending down, Meechum shouldered Reilly and thrust out an arm, parting the ring of farmers to stride purposefully toward the bridge and Painted Rock.

Along the lamplight sprinkled street he walked, his heavy boots thumping the boardwalk.

At the hotel he stopped and looked around. Felix lounged on the saloon porch, his hands tucked beneath the towel tied around his middle. Meechum gave a heave with his shoulder and dumped Reilly noisily on the steps.

Inside, Joanne Avery heard the sound and closed her ledger with a snap. Going to the door, she saw Meechum, his legs spread, an insane anger still gripping him. At the edge of the porch, she looked down at Reilly and gasped, for the lamplight fell full on the young man's face. If she hadn't remembered his new shirt, she would never have recognized him.

When she looked back at Meechum, there was anger churning in her that equaled his own. "Did you do this, Fred?"

"I did," Meechum said. "Tell Frank that's what happens when his kind fools with a decent girl."

"Lottie?"

"Tell him what I said," Meechum repeated.

"I'll tell him," Joanne said tonelessly. "And now I'll tell you something, Fred. You're a yellow dog too scared to fight your own fights. Get out of the country while you can because Owen Frank will kill you for this."

Her words shocked Meechum like a dash of cold water. He stared at her for a long heartbeat, spreading his hands in a silent appeal. "Hell," he said. "I was only protecting her name."

"From what?" Joanne snapped. She flipped her head. "Herb! Come out here and help me." Facing Meechum again she added, "He's a good kid, Fred—better than a man like you deserves for a son-in-law. Who do you think warned Lottie to get you men uptown last night? This boy did. He deserted Alvertone so Owen Frank could clean house for you. Oh, you fool! You blind, dumb fool!"

The clerk came out on the porch, took one look at Reilly and gulped. "Help me with him," Joanne said, and took his feet while Herb lifted the young man by the shoulders. Meechum turned away, walking with stumbling steps like a man in deep shock.

Once they carried Reilly into the lobby, Joanne pushed Herb toward the stairs. "Owen's in his room. Get him down here and hurry."

The clerk's feet beat a quick tattoo on the steps and he hammered loudly on Frank's door. A few moments later, Frank came down the stairs two at a time, tucking in his shirt tail. When he saw Reilly his mouth pulled into a tight line and he said, "Oh, God."

"Herb, go for the doctor," Joanne said, and the clerk ran out and down the street, canted against the blast of the wind. She took Owen's arm. "Can you carry him up-stairs?"

"Sure," Frank said. He lifted Reilly, taking the stairs carefully so as not to trip. Joanne skirted him and went

84

on ahead, opening a door and lighting a lamp. Depositing Reilly gently on the bed, Frank stripped off his shirt and undershirt.

Joanne took a towel and began bathing Reilly's face. Owen saw two wet streaks on her cheeks.

"He'll be all right," Frank said, and touched her shoulder in a light caress. "How did it happen, Joanne? Teepee crew?"

"No. Fred Meechum caught him with Lottie, I guess. He did this to him." She dipped the towel in some water and sponged at Reilly's cuts. She clenched her fist suddenly and beat it against her thigh. "Why, Owen? He didn't deserve this! Not from Meechum."

"You're getting yourself worked up," Frank said. His pale eyes were chilled and there was a rigidness in his cheeks that betrayed the violent feeling that churned within him.

"Where's the right of this?" Joanne asked. "Owen, I thought Burk Alvertone was the cruel one. I thought the farmers were peaceful men."

He shook his head. "Burk's not all bad, nor all good. Neither is Meechum. What he's done, he'll regret." He stopped talking as hurried footsteps rattled on the stairs.

Doctor Harbison entered the room. After one look, he asked, "Did a horse kick him?"

"A man's fist," Frank said. "I think I'll go have a talk with that man." He went out and down the hall. When he came out of his room a few minutes later, he was wearing his gun.

Joanne Avery stood in the doorway, and when he came abreast of her, she raised her hand as if to stop him. But he went past her and down the stairs to the street.

After leaving Burk Alvertone's ranch, the four men settled down to the ride ahead of them. Up in front, Rankin veered to the left, cutting around the sloping end of a mountain to angle toward the position of the old cabin.

The wind, rushing up the slope, swelled in volume to boom among the rocks above them. Rankin swung left again, riding for an hour before he called a halt and dismounted. They took shelter in a thick stand of valley oaks. The wind seemed less here, although it moaned through the upper branches.

"Going to blow up a heller by tomorrow morning," Rankin said to no one in particular. "We'll wait here till after dark," he added in his solid voice. "They'll never know what hit 'em."

"Burk told you to burn the place, that's all," Ace reminded him.

Swinging his head around quickly, Rankin looked intently at the Teepee rider in the gathering gloom. "We'll burn 'em," he said. "Check your guns now."

"We don't need guns," Ace said uneasily. "We need matches."

Turning slowly, Rankin began to crowd Ace. "I'm running this and don't you forget it. And I said check your guns."

"Careful with your pushing," Ace said. "I don't like this none too good anyway."

"Take it easy," Shaw said. "Let's not get to bickering amongst ourselves. The damn weather's enough to set the devil himself on edge."

"You cool off," Rankin advised Ace. "Or I'll have to cool you off myself."

"That might be interesting," Ace muttered, and Shaw pulled at his arm, cautioning him with this small gesture. Ace moved away with Shaw and they squatted by the base of a gnarled tree. Unbuttoning his coat, Ace hunched over to roll a cigarette in the small shelter. He finished it, arced a match to it and settled back.

"Better be careful with him," Shaw whispered. "After what happened at the grove, he don't care who he shoots."

"Calling his bluff would be a pleasure," Ace growled.

"There's lots of time," Shaw said. "After all, Teepee pays us and he's the boss."

"I'm glad you came along, Shaw," Ace said suddenly. He pulled heavily on his smoke and handed it to the other man who took a long pull before passing it back. "Be glad when this job's over," he added. Ace was worried and it showed too plainly to suit him.

Sitting alone, Rankin pillowed his head on his folded arms, his legs tucked under him. Buck stretched out in a long shadow shape on the ground, unmoving and apparently asleep.

When it was fully dark, Rankin rose and stamped his feet to restore the circulation. "Let's go," he said.

"What about a plan?" Buck asked as he sat up.

"We don't need a plan," Rankin said.

"No killing," Ace said. "Fun's fun, but I don't like to think of a killing."

"Damn you!" Rankin began, but then he let it drop. "All right, there'll be shooting but probably no killing. They'll fight some, won't they?"

"Most likely," Ace agreed.

"But they ought to get a chance to run for it," Shaw put in. "Remember that, Rankin—they get a chance to surrender before we put the fire to the place."

"All right," Rankin barked after a short pause. "Now let's get going."

"How do we go in?" Ace asked.

"You and Shaw come in from the sides," Rankin said. "Buck and me'll make our approach from the front and cover the door when they come out. There's no other way out except for the two side windows. Throw a few shots through them when I sing out and they'll probably give up."

"Just be damn careful with the shooting," Ace warned, and climbed into the saddle.

The cabin was less than a mile away, nestled in a bend as the mountain met the valley floor. Keeping to a slow walk, Rankin used a great deal of caution as he approached. He had walked into an ambush last night and did not relish the idea of another.

Three hundred yards away he paused and motioned the others forward with a sweep of his arm. Ace and Shaw rode on ahead, separating to flank the cabin's windows. Rankin waited until they were in position, then edged forward, Buck riding silently beside him.

When they were within fifteen yards of the place, Rankin cupped his hands around his mouth and yelled, "Hey, you! Come out of there or we'll come in after you!"

Almost instantly, a shotgun bellowed and glass shattered from one of the windows as Shaw drove lead into the building. An answering fire commenced from inside and the men on the sides bolted for cover.

At the first volley, Rankin dismounted and drew his revolver, puckering the door panel with three rapid shots. From the side of the cabin, Shaw was doing most of the shooting while Ace lay hidden, content to let the night shroud him.

It was evident that the farmers were holed up together because three guns were going inside the cabin. Buck had circled too far to the right and his horse squealed and went down under him. Cursing, he jumped free and ran back to the front.

Rankin yelled, "All right you dumb cowpoke, go get something to fire it with. We'll smoke the bastards out of there!"

Inside, Oldfield heard this and felt a quick jab of fear. He raised himself to his window and shot once at what he thought was a man, but he knew that he had hit nothing. Over the supper table, Oldfield had made some pretty big talk about how he'd fight off any sonovabitch that tried to run him off. But now, with the fight upon him, his resolve vanished and he wished desperately that he were safely back at the grove, sleeping under a wagon.

On the other side of the room, Hyslip and his son were making a hot fight of it. Several bullets thudded into the wall by their heads but they scarcely seemed to notice. Watching them, Oldfield decided that he had never really known the Hyslips before. They were fighting with a savage intensity.

Somehow, he couldn't quite muster his own courage to that fever pitch.

Once more, Rankin was yelling to someone in his heavy voice, urging him to haste while the wind tossed his words into meaningless sounds. The wind whined through the broken windows and swept the interior of the cabin. It darted into the opening of the fireplace and fanned hot sparks over the floor. Oldfield caught up a bucket of water to splash over them.

"Better save that," Hyslip warned. "They'll put a torch to us in a little while. We'll need it then."

"We got to get out of here," Oldfield panted. He couldn't mask the panic in his voice.

"Easy now," Hyslip cautioned. "There's four of 'em, I think. They've got the edge now, but the walls are stout and we have plenty of shells."

This failed to reassure Oldfield, although he returned to his window and scanned the dark land. For some reason, there was no firing on his side. He wondered if anyone was out there, and decided that there must be. Some cool man who waited, saving his ammunition, hoping that a farmer would try to dart through. The thought of dying filled Oldfield with terror.

Rankin was like a wild man in his haste to set fire to the cabin. From the leanto barn, Buck brought hay, but five attempts to light it failed in the stout wind.

Cursing him, Rankin ordered him to the shelter of the barn. With a screening wall to aid him, Buck finally got a pitchfork load of hay aflame. But when he made a dash with it across the yard, the wind whipped it off the tines, scattering it in a brilliant shower.

Shaw was stationed near the window guarded by Hyslip and his son. He crouched in the brush, content to lie low while the Hyslips shot at anything they thought might be a man. On the other side, Ace lay belly flat, wondering why there was no more shooting from the window he covered. In the beginning the firing had been wicked and blindly aimed but now there was no sign of life. As he had not yet fired, he felt reasonably certain that the man had not been hit, unless an early bullet had caught him from the other side.

Near the barn, Buck made another fruitless attempt to carry a forkful of fire across the yard. The wind ruined it as before. Five trips he made, carrying armfuls of hay to stack against the side of the cabin, crawling along on his belly so that the Hyslips couldn't see him.

By opening his coat as a shield he managed to ignite the hay, but even as it began to burn well the wind whipped it away from the wall, scattering it dangerously near the dried brush where Shaw lay hidden.

There seemed no chance for success. Dry, the hay did not scatter too badly, but once lit and partially consumed, it became a fickle toy of the wind. Guarding the front door, Rankin fumed because the cabin still was not in flames.

"Go to hell then!" Buck yelled angrily. "Fire it yourself!"

"Damn it, you fire it!" Rankin told him. "Use your head. Get yourself a pole and heave it through the window."

Buck went back to the barn to see what he could find. An old spring wagon sat along the far side, hidden from his view until he went around in back. An idea mauled him and he began to load hay in the back of it. When he had a large pile he arced another match and touched it off.

It took all his strength to push it but Rankin helped him the last twenty yards and they edged it close alongside the cabin wall beneath the Hyslips' window. The wind plucked at the hay, whirling some through the natural flue the window provided, but the bulk of it burned feebly and was flung aloft without igniting the logs.

In a short time the wagon was burned down to the four steel rims, the hubs and a few iron fittings. The tongue remained, however, and with this, Buck fashioned a long prod with a bundle of hay tied around the lighter end. He finally got it ignited and with Rankin's help, lifted it and poked it through the window.

Someone inside dashed a bucket of water on it and it went out. Rankin cursed in insane fury.

"Keep it up!" Buck yelled. "Hell, they don't have a well in there. They'll run out of water pretty soon!"

"That's right," Rankin admitted, calming his wrath. "Get some more hay."

Running to the barn, Buck fetched another armful and again they tied a bundle to the end of the tongue. Since the front of the cabin was just blank logs, it was not dangerous for them to approach boldly. But they had to stay around the front corner as they manipulated the tongue with its fiery tip to the window.

This time there was no water, for young Hyslip stuck his head and shoulders out and shot splinters from the log by Rankin's head. The foreman had a desperate courage. He leaped into the open and fanned his gun empty. But young Hyslip had ducked back and the bullets just shaved wood from the window sill.

"Get another load," Rankin ordered, and again Buck trotted to the barn.

This time Rankin had a new strategy to try. "Get set," he said as Buck lighted the hay with some difficulty. "Now, stick it in there!" Rankin yelled, and then jumped away from the wall for a clear shot at the window. He pulled his other gun and rolled the hammer, keeping the Hyslips down as Buck manipulated the burning hay inside.

A sudden yelp went up as the wind fanned the fire throughout the interior. Rankin grinned. "Get some more," he said.

Buck cursed disgustedly. He was ready to call it off, but one look at Rankin told him that nothing short of death would stop him from firing the place.

Three trips later, the fire inside the cabin was out of control. They could see the leaping flames through the side windows as Oldfield and the Hyslips fought it with blankets.

This seemed to satisfy Rankin, for he called Ace and Shaw to him. They gathered in a knot by the front door to await the farmers' surrender.

"Come on out!" Rankin yelled.

"Come out and get killed?" Hyslip called back. "We're not that crazy."

"Stay in there and burn then, if you want to!" Rankin said. "You haven't got much time to make up your mind!"

He stood spraddle-legged with the wind rocking him, shoving fresh shells into his guns. Ace and Shaw were a few yards to the left. Buck remained on Rankin's right side, his attention on the tall man, not on the cabin.

Inside, the Hyslips and Oldfield put up a valiant battle against the growing fire, but it was a losing fight. The wind howling through the broken windows created a perfect draft and the logs caught quickly, burning with an ever increasing heat.

Rankin seemed to sense their growing distress. He yelled, "Last call! Come out with your hands up!"

"All right," Oldfield called. "I'm throwing out my gun. So's the Hyslips." From a side window a rifle and two shotguns thudded into the grass.

The front door opened a crack, shooting out a shaft of firelight. The elder Hyslip stepped out, his hands upraised, followed by his son. There was a commotion along the far side and Oldfield hit the ground running. "Go get him!" Rankin snapped at Shaw and Ace, not taking his eyes from the Hyslips who waited before the open door, eerily silhouetted against the red fury behind them.

"Suckers," Rankin said.

He raised his gun and shot the old man squarely in the chest. His second shot cut young Hyslip down.

For a stunned instant, neither Ace nor Shaw moved, but Buck did not show any surprise.

Rankin watched the two men fall, remaining absolutely

motionless, his gun still held hip high. "That's a lesson to all men with a yearning for Teepee grass," he said savagely. Striding forward, he turned young Hyslip over with his toe. "Get mounted. The job's done."

CHAPTER 8

Once clear of the burning cabin, Oldfield sought the cover of the brush on the east side, hunkering down as two shots cracked the windy night. He listened carefully, wishing he had not discarded his shotgun. A wild fear screamed through him that the Teepee men would search him out.

The shock of his first fright was wearing thin now and a dull shame began to grip him. The cabin burned fiercely, the wind whipping sparks across the land in a wild display. One wall collapsed with a pounding roar.

Oldfield thrashed his way through the brush, counting on the crash of the wind to drown out the sounds of his movement. When he had edged around far enough to command a view of the front, he saw the huddled forms of the Hyslips on the ground but no sign of the Teepee men.

Ten minutes later, Oldfield summoned enough courage to leave the security of the thicket and approach the cabin. He stared at young Hyslip, lying face up, his arms outstretched. His peaked hat had fallen free and now the wind pushed it playfully across the yard. In the fire's glare, Oldfield saw the young man's hair ruffle; it was the only movement.

Oldfield crossed the yard to the collapsed barn and found that the two teams were still there, as were their wagons. Hitching them slowly in the darkness, he tied Hyslip's team to his tailgate and led them to the cabin.

The fury of the fire had died down, and with it the red glare. The wind tore sparks from the glowing coals and the fireplace stood gaunt and lonely in the night light.

Lifting the body of the older man, Oldfield laid him

gently in the back of the wagon, then went back for Hyslip's son. With his friends side by side, Oldfield mounted the front wagon, his own, and drove from the yard.

His mind was heavy with regret and old sorrows returned to plague him. From Oldfield's viewpoint, life had never been fruitful. The ingrained decency in the man dictated that he return his friends to the grove for burial, even though he dreaded the withering scorn of the others for his cowardice.

Had he been more acute he would have realized that they shared his weaknesses and therefore would understand. For among them there were no successful farmers, but rather men who were accustomed to defeat. Misfits and castoffs, they were migrating in search of that oasis of plenty that existed only in their minds.

He drove into the black night, hunched over on the wagon seat while the relentless wind blasted him, billowing the canvas top and bending the lush grass beneath its heavy hand.

Fred Meechum hated mistakes, and now he understood dully that he had committed his most serious one by beating Reilly. His fears, like those of most men, were deep rooted, having their origin in an experience many years past.

Perhaps he hated the thought of any man touching his daughter because he could recall so vividly his own impulsive youth and the intemperate passion that had eaten like an acid at his vitals. This had driven him to an early and ill chosen marriage and with his severe upbringing there was no hope for correcting this act. All his life he had looked with envy on men who could find virtue in a cheap woman, understanding vaguely that they had enough humanity to overlook weakness and see only the good.

Unfortunately, Fred Meechum had never been able to do that.

Approaching his own fire now, he found his wife huddled near the blaze while Lottie took sanctuary in the wagon, the sound of her weeping audible below the shriek of the wind in the trees.

Standing with his heavy legs widespread, Meechum stared at his wife, then said bleakly, "I should have known

93

she'd turn out like you. I've watched for it ever since she began to fill out."

"Blame me," the woman snapped, raising her head. "That's all you ever did—blame me. You think I dragged you down, don't you?" She laughed mockingly, her face twisted and without mirth. "The good Lord's getting back at you for the way you've treated me, Fred Meechum."

"Don't talk to me of the Lord's wrath!" he said venomously. "You were a lying, tricky slut and I married you." He bent forward and threw a chunk of wood on the fire. "Agh, what's the use of hashing over what's past. We'll have our land soon and she'll live this down. I'll hear of no man speaking of it!" He doubled one fist before him.

"There's no land here for us," she said bitterly. "Nothing's the same as you promised me. Everything you touch goes to pieces—even her. But I'm not going to stand for that, you hear? I've told her she can go if she wants to."

"You told her what?" Meechum's eyes grew round and his whole expression was one of disbelief. "See here, you're taking something on yourself that's not yours to decide. She's my kid and she'd better do as I say. When I want her to marry, she'll marry. No man better come smelling around before, either."

His wife stared at him, the firelight glistening on her fat face. Then she began to laugh, a dry, humorless cackle that made the flesh jiggle on her heavy arms.

"What's so funny?" he asked, his temper returning in force.

"I'm thinking of you, you big fool," she said, and stood up. "You've never loved me and you've never loved Lottie either. You don't know how to love things, Fred. You just want to own 'em. Only this time I'm holding the trump, one I've been saving for years." She stepped around the fire and thrust her face close to his. "She ain't yours, you hear? She never was yours!"

For a stunned heartbeat, Meechum stared back at his wife. Then his arm came up almost automatically and he struck her with his fist, hurling her backward. She hit the wagon wheel and slumped heavily, but when she raised her head she was laughing with a terrible, silent laughter. In a moment her expression changed and she bent forward, crying in a lost and heartbroken way.

Meechum stared at her and then lifted his fist, looking for a long time at the knuckles. Someone called to him from across the camp and his head swiveled in that direction.

He recognized the tall shape of Owen Frank striding toward him, and reached for his shotgun.

Most of the families stayed near their own wagons and the cookfires fed sparks to the wind that whipped up through the trees, lifting dust from the hoof-chopped compound.

Meechum squatted down by his fire, his shotgun across his knees. His wife saw Frank and crawled to the rear of the wagon, peering around the huge rear wheel as the Texan approached.

Rising slowly, Meechum brought the shotgun across his chest. He was ready, yet somewhat uncertain of what was in Owen Frank's mind. When fifteen yards separated them, Owen Frank said, "Point that at me and you're a dead man." The wind distorted his words, but Fred Meechum raised the shotgun no further.

Skirting Meechum's fire, Frank halted before the man, knocked the shotgun from his hands, and kicked it under the wagon.

"Where's the girl?" he asked.

Meechum nodded toward the wagon. "In there."

"Get Lottie out here."

"She's my girl and I say what she does when it pleases me," Meechum said.

"I won't tell you again," Frank murmured, and the firelight made dancing spots of light in his eyes.

Meechum turned and rapped on the wagon box. Lottie came out slowly, her eyes red from crying, her face smeared. In the scuffle with her parents, her dress had been torn on one shoulder and her hair was loose and disheveled.

The farmers began to leave their wagons and sift across the compound, the women and children following close behind. They circled Meechum's fire, watching and listening but saying nothing.

Meechum's wife stood beside Lottie, holding the girl's arm.

"Turn her loose," Frank said.

Meechum's wife made no move and the big man snapped, "You heard what he said, dammit!" The woman released

95

Lottie and the girl sank to her knees in the dust, her loose hair whipping in the wind. After looking at her for what seemed a long time, Owen Frank raised his eyes to Fred Meechum.

"You're a worthless dog," he said softly. "You're good at laying for a man, or jumping a kid. When I started here I intended to drive you from the grove."

Meechum's face hardened but he made no move to fight. "What business is this of yours anyway?" he asked. "Seems like a man ought to be able to protect his family without interference."

"Just don't say nothing to me, Meechum," Frank warned. "Just don't say a damn word, you understand?" He looked down at Lottie and found her watching him. "Did Reilly bother you, Lottie?"

She shook her head dumbly. "He never touched me," she said finally, and glared at her father. "We just sat and talked because he was lonely." She got up from the dusty ground and stepped around the fire to Owen Frank's side. "I'm going to him," she told her father defiantly. "I'll say good-bye too because I'm never coming back."

"You don't mean that," Meechum said. "You're mad at your old dad now, but tomorrow you'll feel different." He reached out a hand as though to touch her and she recoiled. "I know what your ma told you and I don't hold it against you none. I've always been a good pa to you, haven't I?" Meechum's eyes swept the solid ring of faces but saw none of them. He looked back at the girl appealingly. "I intended no harm, girl. But when I saw him with you I got to thinkin' about myself, I guess. When I was young. You got to understand what it is to be a man, what he thinks."

"How would you know what Reilly thinks?" Lottie said. "He's good, you understand—good." Turning to Frank, she asked, "Where is he now?"

"At the hotel. The doctor and Joanne are with him." He took her arm, halting her as she started to move away. "He won't look the same any more, girl."

"He's the same inside," she said, and looked at her parents. "Good-bye," she told them, and then she elbowed her way through the crowd around the fire. A moment later she was running from the grove toward Painted Rock.

Meechum's wife watched her out of sight, then whirled on her husband, striking him in the mouth with her

96

clenched fist. "You and your stiff-necked ways! I'm sick of it. Sick of all this fancy pretendin' about being something that you ain't!" Her face started to crumple then, and she buried it in her hands as she stumbled off by herself.

At the perimeter of the camp, the rattle of wagons overrode the scuff of the wind and a man called out in a loud, demanding voice. Some of the people turned away from Meechum as the wagon drew nearer, the noise of its passage clear and pronounced now. The circle of faces began to fan out and Will Savage broke through, glancing first at Owen Frank and then at Meechum.

"There's been some trouble," he said.

Meechum shrugged. "I don't want to hear about it. I have enough of my own." He walked away, leaving the sheriff standing there. The team stopped and Oldfield dismounted stiffly and approached the group. Spreading his hands over the fire, he stood silently.

A lanky man crossed to the back wagon and discovered the Hyslips. His shout broke up the gathering and they all crowded around the wagon. One man ran for a lantern and several mounted the bed, removing Hyslip and his son to the ground.

Detaching himself from the others, Jim Clover came over. Since that night in Owen Frank's room, Clover had kept to the background; but with Meechum's sudden withdrawal from leadership, he hoped to edge his way in.

The sudden death of the Hyslips had a stunning effect on the farmers, proving beyond all doubt Alvertone's method of dealing with squatters. The earlier victory over Teepee seemed insignificant in the face of this catastrophe.

All of them wanted free land, but not at the risk of a bullet.

Clover said, "Savage, I demand that something be done about this."

"Are you running things now?" Savage asked.

"If no one else wants the responsibility, I'll take it."

"No one's going to take it," Savage snapped, and looked around to see who objected. "Owen, I'm placing the blame of all this on you. If you hadn't been so damn proud you couldn't pass up a fight, this never would have happened."

"You damned idiot!" Frank exploded. "This was blowing up in your face. Couldn't you see it?"

"The blowup hasn't come yet, my wise friend. Wait

until Alvertone finds out the election is scheduled for to-morrow. This town won't be safe for a farmer to show his face." Savage made a disgusted motion with his hand and turned to Clover. "Get the Hyslips laid out for burial. We'll hold the service in the morning."

"We got no preacher with us," Clover said.

"I'll get Hy Linnet at the Wells Fargo office," the sheriff said. "He reads the Bible all the time." Bending over Meechum's fire, Savage helped himself to a cup of coffee and drank it slowly.

The two wagons were led away and unhitched, while the farmers dispersed, wanting time to think this out. Owen Frank hunkered down on his haunches and studied them, drawing a comparison between these farmers and cattle-men. He guessed it was the nature of their occupations that nurtured their difference in thinking. A cowboy lived a precarious existence, for his work was inherently dangerous and sudden violence was taken as a matter of course.

But the farmers lived a sedate life, hardworking, yes, but not dangerous. Over the years their thinking paced itself to their routine, monotonous and somewhat plodding. They grew slow to anger and uncertain of what to do when in anger.

He had observed this variance in disposition before, while watching a farmer and a cowboy fight. The farmer was really whipped before he began, for deep down lay his reluctance to injure another. The cowboy had no such notion and while the farmer merely fended him off, the cowboy got in his vicious licks and the fight was over. Could a man say that the cattleman was the better scrapper? Frank decided that even though he might be inferior, he had ruthlessness and that was what counted in a fight.

Studying Will Savage, Frank wondered if beneath it all the sheriff was not more farmer than cattleman. He lacked the drive demanded by his office. From the beginning Will Savage had tried to appease both sides, an impossibility from Owen Frank's point of view. Even now he kept trying to straddle the fence when everyone could see that it was too late.

Frank could find no real blame for Will Savage; he just didn't have the brass to carry it off. It took a man who could bully farmers and cattlemen alike so that both kept the peace.

Savage was for the farmers to the extent that he would allow no unnecessary bloodshed, but he would not sanction their moving on Teepee grass, nor would he protect them if they did. He was faced with a hopeless situation and like a blind man lost on an unfamiliar street, he groped and fumbled, but could not find a way out.

Alvertone probably hoped to discourage the farmers by killing Hyslip and his son, and for the moment, he had. But tomorrow the numbness would wear away and the farmers would be more determined than ever.

Especially if Will Savage won the election. Well, Frank had resolved that he would.

Throwing what was left of his coffee into the fire, Savage rose and said, "Frank, I'd like to have a little talk with you—in my office."

"All right," Owen murmured, and stood up. Meechum was content to stare silently at the fire, ignoring them as they left the grove.

Crossing the bridge, Savage said, "You were a fool to interfere with Meechum and his daughter. I thought you had better sense than that."

"The time to be sensible is past." Frank pulled up his coat collar against the battering wind. "You better do this my way, Will. Save time in the long run."

They passed the hotel and were near the corner when Savage answered. "With a gun, Frank?" He shook his head, inserting a key in the lock. When he closed the door the moan of the wind was muffled. Savage lighted a lamp. "Have a seat. No, I can't go along with you. Alvertone rode on the grove because of what you did to him and Sweikert the other night. If you hadn't batted him around, he wouldn't have exploded. Of course things got out of hand then. After the farmers ran the Teepee men off they got to feeling big and had to move out. Hyslip and his boy are the first, but that was something Alvertone figured he had to do, Frank. Had things been left alone in the first place, it wouldn't have happened."

Hoisting his feet to the edge of Savage's desk, Frank rolled a cigarette, bending over the lamp for his light. "You're like a man trying to weigh gold dust in a wind," he said. "You're wearing yourself out trying to keep everything even when it can't be done. If Alvertone hits a farmer, you want to see him get paid back, but only hard enough to even it up again." Frank shook his head. "That fence you've been walking is going to crack, Will. It's a long fall to the ground."

"You're wrong," Savage insisted with his lock-jawed stubbornness. "I'm going to win this election, Owen, and when Alvertone sees that he's going to give in a little. Oh, I know he's not going to open his arms to the farmers, but there'll be a truce. You'll see."

Frank shied his smoke into the stove and walked to the door. "Will, I like you. Even when you're a damn fool. I hope you're right about Burk Alvertone. I surely do."

He opened the door and went out, head lowered into the wind. Mounting the hotel porch, Frank entered the lobby and stopped in surprise, for in spite of the late hour a fair-sized crowd had gathered here. They stood quiet-faced with an air of expectancy about them.

Spotting Hy Linnet by the desk, Frank asked in a low voice, "What's the matter, Hy?"

"Gus had another spell," Linnet said, and chewed on an unlighted cigar. "The doc's in with him now."

"Where's Joanne?"

"In her room." Linnet raised his eyes to Frank's. "He may not last, Owen. See if you can talk to her. She wouldn't let anyone in."

"All right," Frank agreed, and went to the stairs. Pausing there, he singled out a man in the crowd and said, "Better get Will Savage." The man nodded and hurried out as Frank ascended the stairs.

Knocking at Joanne's door, he waited several minutes before knocking again. "Who is it?" she asked.

"Owen Frank."

Finally he heard her move and the bolt slid back. He opened the door and went inside, leaning his back against it after he had closed it. She kept her back turned toward him. Her shoulders hunched as if she were cold, although a strong fire sang in the pot-bellied stove.

"I couldn't stay with him any longer," she whispered. "I couldn't listen to him talk." She sat down in a deep, wing-back chair and clasped her hands together. The lamplight gilded the smooth skin of her face. Tears welled up in her eyes and glistened for a moment along her bottom lids before spilling over to run down her cheeks. But the composure of her face never broke.

"He isn't sorry he's going to die, Owen. He's sorry for me because he thinks I haven't learned how to enjoy life. He blames himself for that."

"He isn't blaming anyone," Frank said. "Gus is too smart for that. Only fools sit around and blame each other. He's just sorry that some things aren't different, just as you're sorry now that you aren't quite how he wanted you to be."

She glanced at him quickly. "How would you know about that?" she asked in a soft voice.

Frank shrugged his shoulders slightly. "He never wanted you to mother him, Joanne, but you did. He didn't want to be the man in your life. A woman isn't built that way. That's what he's sorry about."

Slowly she lowered her head and stared at her folded hands. Outside, the wind rocketed against the siding, shaking the building slightly with its unrelenting fury. Finally she vacated her chair and moved to the door.

"I want to go back now," she said softly, and Owen Frank opened the door for her and trailed her down the stairs. They crossed the lobby and entered the back room.

Gus Avery was very pale against the sheets, but when he saw the tears on Joanne's cheeks he smiled and took her hand. Doctor Harbison was closing his bag, shaking his head gently.

"I've never seen you cry," Gus said in a whisper. "Not since the day your mother died. Crying's good for you, girl."

"I know," Joanne told him.

"This is an easier road than I figured," Gus said. "For a long time it scared me, but not any more." He patted her hand. "You'll be all right now, honey."

"I'll be all right," she said.

The old man's eyes grew hazy and he looked at Owen Frank standing against the wall. "Don't be a fool now, girl. You got your man so forget about the other nonsense. Nothin's so important as bein' with him. There ain't much else you have to know about livin' if you love someone."

He rolled his head on the pillow and his breathing deepened, a strong, gusty sawing in the room. For a full minute he stared at the ceiling, his eyes vague and introspective, and then in the last moment some humor came into his face and he looked at his daughter. "I don't hear no damned angels," he said, and his breath left him in a long sigh.

Joanne sat there for some time, then leaned forward and stroked his brow. Rising from the edge of the bed, she walked over to Owen Frank, her face controlled, but when she touched him the damn broke and she went into his arms crying unrestrainedly.

Frank made a slight motion with his head and the doctor, went out. Frank held Joanne gently until her sobbing subsided and when she stirred in his arms she had regained control of herself again.

The door opened suddenly and Will Savage halted on the threshold. In one glance he saw that he was too late. Closing the door, he touched Joanne on the arm and said, "I'm sorry."

"He wasn't sorry," she murmured. "In a way, I think he was relieved. He disliked being a burden. I think that was his strongest trait, his independence."

"I'll take care of everything," Savage said, and stared at Frank. The sheriff's eyes held a resentment that he could not conceal. Opening the door quietly, Frank let himself out and went up the stairs to Reilly's room.

Joanne gazed steadily at the door Frank had just closed, and this added to Savage's uneasiness.

"Is it like that?" he asked heavily.

"Is it like what?" Her voice was cool and slightly distant.

"You don't want him, Joanne. He'll break your heart." He threw his hat in a chair and took her shoulders, forcing her to look at him. "Joanne, listen to me. I know Owen Frank—he's a drifter. You saw how he came to this town, with nowhere to go and nothing left he cared about. Do you think you're the only woman he's known? He's not for you. When this trouble's over, he'll say good-bye and never give you another thought. That's his way, Joanne. He'll not change."

"Maybe I'll change," she said. "Did you ever think of that?"

"I've thought of it," Savage said. "You're not fooling me, Joanne. Just yourself. Before you came here, your father led you from pillar to post with no real home to go back to. You got him to stop here, and now that you have your roots down you wouldn't pull them up for any man. You can't change your way of living any more than he can, and you know it."

"Please, leave me alone," she said. "Go, Will—I mean it."

"All right," he said. "I'll always be around, Joanne. You can count on that."

He waited for an answer but she had none for him. When he realized this he opened the door and went out, leaving her alone with her father.

Joanne lifted the sheet over Gus's head, covering him completely, and then turned down the lamp until there was only a soft glow in the room. She moved through the shadows and went out, closing the door softly as if he were just sleeping and she had no wish to disturb him.

She mounted the stairs, wondering how Owen Frank understood her need so clearly. He was like a wind blowing strong and clean, leaving a breathless suspense in its wake. If she chose his life there could be no security or peace, for he was a restless wanderer but she could find no desire in her heart to change him.

Surprisingly, her logic was not very effective for she loved him and that in itself was a powerful force pulling at her reason. Her father's words had a ring of truth: if you loved a man you had everything.

She wanted to believe this, but the voice of habit was strong within her, drowning it out.

Passing Reilly's room, she heard Owen Frank's soft drawl and suppressed the urge to enter and be near him. Forcing herself on to her own room, she closed the door and leaned against it. She could detect a faint trace of tobacco and leather and an overwhelming sorrow engulfed her. In that moment she realized that even after he rode away he would not really be gone, for a man like him left his mark behind him on everything he touched.

She began to weep again, this time in silent despair.

CHAPTER 9

Lottie Meechum answered Owen Frank's soft knock. There was a small lamp by the bed, pooling light on the young man. His face was hidden by bandages and he asked, "Who is it? Speak up."

"It's me, kid," Frank said, and saw Reilly relax beneath the covers. Lottie gave Frank her chair and perched on the edge of the bed. The young man moved his hand aimlessly over the quilt, toying with the tufts. "Make her go back, Owen. You can see she's got to, can't you?"

"I don't like to stick my nose in other people's business," Frank said. "Since I came here, I've done nothing but that and I'm pondering the wisdom of it." He shook out a sack of tobacco and rolled a cigarette. After lighting it, he handed it to Reilly, who puffed gratefully.

"I've been thinking," Frank continued, "that you didn't put up too good a show against Meechum. Didn't you want to hit him?"

"I wanted to," Reilly admitted. "I wanted to stomp a hole in his head, but there wasn't nothing to be gained by that." He puffed on the smoke and handed it back to Owen Frank, fumbling blindly until he found the tall Texan's hand. "From the beginning it was no good," he went on. "But sometimes a man sees something and he can't help himself. I wanted to be friendly with Meechum on account of his daughter. Hitting him wouldn't have brought me any closer."

"Suppose she goes away with you, Reilly. Will she always be happy?"

"I'll be happy," Lottie said defensively.

"For a while," Frank agreed. "But time changes things and some day you'll wonder where your folks are and there won't be any way you can find out. Then you'll start regretting and it'll turn on you and make you sour."

"You can see why she's got to go back," Reilly said. "Owen, make her go back to the grove."

"I won't go back," Lottie said. "Pa can come to me. He's spent a lifetime making people come to him. Now a little switch around won't hurt him." She studied Owen Frank seriously. "You know, I think you're going to lose too. It bothers you because you don't like to lose. It's your pride that makes you want a woman to go your way completely. You might find a woman like that some day, but you won't be happy with her because that isn't what you want at all."

The tall Texan stroked his mustache with a forefinger.

"You don't want this girl to go back, Reilly," he said, and slapped his thighs before rising.

Crossing to the door, he paused with his hand on the brass knob. "Gus Avery died a few minutes ago," he said, and went out.

The crowd had dispersed from the lobby. He passed through to stand on the arcade. The wind had increased in velocity and now it bore the unmistakable odor of rain. As he stood there listening to a sign squeal two doors down, a large drop splattered in the dusty street, and then another, until the air held a slanting sheet of water. It drummed on the porch roof and the eaves began to gurgle noisily as they filled up and spilled down the drain pipes.

The saloon was still open and Frank stepped from the porch to cross over, a hundred tiny mallets pelting the felt crown of his hat. As he entered, he removed his hat and slapped it against his thigh. The water showered off in sparkling droplets.

Three farmers sat against the far wall playing cards. Frank eyed them curiously, recognizing the tension that held them here. Behind the bar, Felix grinned and raised a bottle and glass. Frank walked gingerly over the freshly sawdusted floor, glancing back at his tracks. He leaned against the bar and said, "Seems a shame to mess it up, doesn't it?"

"That's life," Felix said. "Seems like every time a man gets things pretty much to suit him, someone always comes along to plow right through it."

He poured two drinks and Frank up-ended his glass. Nodding toward the three farmers, he murmured, "They're up kind of late, aren't they?"

"The country's comin' apart at the seams," Felix said, and smiled. "They don't want to miss any of it. Will Savage was in here a while ago. He's worried about the election."

"Let's worry about it in the morning when the polls open," Frank said. "Let's have another, Felix. That was pretty good." He nursed the second one a little. "You hear what happened down at the grove?"

"Too bad. But then some people just got to stick their finger in the bear trap to see if it's set."

"Alvertone's playing for keeps," Frank said. "He'll play that way tomorrow."

"Doc Harbison said that Sweikert's up and around now,"

Felix said. "I look for the whole crew in any time." He paused while Owen Frank polished off his drink. "Have another?"

"Two's plenty," Frank said, and glanced at the wall clock. "Ten-thirty. Burk knows about the election date being set up?"

"Doc Harbison mentioned it. He says Burk hit the ceiling." Felix tried to laugh off his worries. "Harbison claims Burk swears he'll take the damn town apart tomorrow."

"He may just do that," Frank admitted ruefully, and scratched his ear. He glanced over his shoulder at the three farmers, then swung his attention to the door as four more came in. Each man carried a shotgun or rifle. When they ordered their beers, they laid the guns on the bar within easy reach.

Frank remained at the bar after the farmers took their beers and guns to a table. At eleven o'clock Will Savage came in. His face grew more worried when he saw the farmers' weapons.

Taking a place by Frank's elbow, he ordered a whisky and tossed it off.

"Still raining?" Frank asked, eyeing Savage's wet slicker.

"Like thunder," Savage said, and cradled the glass in his hands. He shook his head slowly. "This is going to be a bad night all the way around."

"Burk Alvertone's coming in," Frank said quietly.

"I know. Doc Harbison told me when we took Gus Avery to him." The sheriff slapped the bar impatiently and his handsome face was severe. New lines had formed around his eyes and he carried a pinched look at the ends of his lips. "Dammit, I'm no gunfighter. How can I hold Alvertone's crew back?"

"Worry about it tomorrow," Frank said. "They'll drink and raise a little hell tonight, but the lid won't come off until tomorrow." He raised his eyes to the wall clock again. "Felix tells me Sweikert is back on his feet. I guess I didn't hit him hard enough."

"That's where we differ," Savage said. "I say you shouldn't have hit him at all." He waved his hands. "What's the use of arguing now? The fat's in the fire and we might as well get used to the idea."

"There never was any argument," Frank said. "Alvertone decided he was going to be the big boss and everyone went along with it. Now there's been some mind changing but nobody wants to tell him so."

Savage snorted. "You think these farmers are going to be better for the country than Alvertone? If Fred Meechum and Clover are good examples, then I wonder."

"It'll be better," Frank insisted, "because they'll never get organized and they don't use guns to settle their differences. Cattlemen are in the habit of working together. First ·there were the Indians, and then the rustlers, and now the farmers. The farmers have always played a lone hand. A country's more peaceful with them. I wish you could see it in time."

"You talk funny for a cattleman," Savage said. "Somehow I can't see Alvertone breaking to the outside of the law."

"He already has," Frank commented. "The Hyslips."

"Let's put that down as a desperate man backing his own convictions," Will said. "I'm talking about Alvertone's defiance of my authority. He won't do that. He never has in the past and there's no reason for him to do it tomorrow."

"The past and tomorrow are two different things," Frank said. "In the past you were a cattleman sheriff in cattle country. Now it's different."

"I'll agree to that," Felix put in. "Will, why don't you pin a badge on Frank and play this careful."

"No thanks," Will said stiffly. "I'm not hiring a gun to enforce the law. That's not the way to settle this—ramming justice down anyone's throat. Burk will see it my way."

Sighing, Owen Frank nodded at Felix and said, "I think I will have another drink, after all." He crossed his hands while Felix poured, glancing over his shoulder as the front door opened wide. Burk Alvertone and half his crew stomped in.

The farmers at the tables ceased talking, leaving no sound in the room except the muffled blast of rain against the building. Felix said, "Close the damn door. There's a draught in here."

The door banged shut and Alvertone and his men moved deeper into the room, their spurs setting up an ominous tinkle on the sawdust-covered floor. Alvertone and his fifteen men bellied against the bar, unbuckling their slickers.

Most of them wore visible bruises from the grove fight,

while others sported bandages around their heads. Alvertone banged on the bar for service, but never took his eyes from Frank and Savage.

Going along with his bottle, Felix filled glasses and came back. The Teepee hands remained quiet but there was a dancing light in Alvertone's eyes that couldn't be ignored.

"Where's Sweikert?" Savage asked. "Didn't he come in with you?"

"He's in," Alvertone said. "Over at the hotel. He heard about Reilly and wanted to see how he was getting along."

Savage frowned and Frank moved away from the bar, but Alvertone held up his hand. "Careful now, gunfighter. You're not going any place."

"You going to stop me?"

"There's fifteen guns here," Alvertone said. "We'll stop you."

A series of dry clicks pulled Alvertone's face around. He found himself staring into the muzzle of a double-barreled shotgun. Felix said, "This ain't your night, Burk."

There was no fear in the old man. He laced his hands together on the bar, throwing his weight on his elbows. "Put that away, Felix, and I'll let this pass."

"No play," Felix said. "The first man that reaches, you get both barrels right in the face."

"Don't play tough with me," Alvertone said tightly. "Damn it, I'll run you out of the country with a bare butt!"

"Tomorrow maybe, but not tonight," Felix told him. "Mind me now, Burk. Get your boys to put their hands on the cherrywood."

One of the farmers at the tables cocked his shotgun. It was the signal for others to ready their weapons and point them at the Teepee riders. One young man exhibited a crack in his nerve as he said, "Hell!" in a high, nervous voice.

"Better do as he says, cattleman," a tall farmer said, and hit the spittoon with a stream of tobacco without looking at it.

Alvertone's lips pulled down tightly behind his mustache. His men placed their hands on the bar and waited. Felix said, "You know, I'm particular who I sell to. The drinks were on the house. Don't bother to come back for more."

Glancing at Owen Frank, he nodded slightly and the tall

Texan moved toward the door. Savage remained unmoving, taking no part in this.

The door opened and closed and Owen Frank left the porch, head down agaisnt the driving rain. He splashed across the muddy street and took the hotel steps two at a time. He opened the front door as the rolling blast of gunfire rattled the building.

Alone in her room, Joanne Avery sat before the fire and listened to the pelt of rain as it rattled on the window and set up a constant chatter on the roof.

When she heard Owen Frank leave the hotel, she felt an almost uncontrollable urge to call after him and bring him back. Then she reasoned that he had left her alone deliberately. Understanding how deep her pride was, he had given her this time alone to straighten out her thoughts.

In him there was something solid and reassuring; she had felt it the first time she talked to him. His arms had been a haven in her first moment of grief, but now he had withdrawn to allow her to see that no one could lean for long on another. Tomorrow was a fact that she would have to face alone and unafraid, and if she felt misgivings she could not show them to anyone, not even him.

The small watch pinned to her dress indicated that it was after eleven-thirty so she went downstairs to close the hotel. Through the front windows she watched the rain sheer off the slanting porch in a silver sheet where the lamplight touched it.

Above the moan of the storm she heard the plod of many horses and moved closer to the window. Alvertone's men pulled up before the saloon and dismounted. Among the shifting shapes she recognized Sweikert, and her interest sharpened. Once under the shelter of the saloon overhang, Burk Alvertone drew Sweikert to one side, talking rapidly. When she saw him gesture toward an upstairs window in the hotel, Joanne felt the first thrust of fear and went to the desk where she kept a gun.

When Sweikert tramped across the front porch, Joanne slid the small .38 out of the drawer and held it beneath the counter.

The door opened and Sweikert came in, slapping his hat against his leg. For a moment she was appalled at the damage Owen Frank had inflicted with his fists. Both eyes were still puffed to mere slits and the discoloration had spread to his cheekbones. Sweikert's bottom lip was twice its normal size and the cut flesh on one cheekbone looked raw and infected.

He gave her a wolfish grin and paced across the floor, leaving a wet trail behind him. When he approached the desk he slipped out of his slicker and laid it over the blotter, soaking the pad.

She glanced down distastefully and brushed the hat off to the floor. "Leave your bunkhouse manners outside when you come in here," she said.

This made him laugh. He looked her over carefully, deliberately dropping his eyes to the swell of her breasts. When he raised his eyes to hers again she had her fear under control and her expression was cool. "Looking is free," she told him. "But touch me and you'll get hurt."

"Now you wouldn't hurt a man, would you?" He tried a smile and then gave it up. His pearl handled guns had been replaced by a pair of walnut butted Colts and he shrugged these around to the crown of his hips. "Tell me something, honey—is Reilly in one of those upstairs rooms?"

"Maybe."

"Maybe nothin'," he said. "He's there. His horse is in the stable down the street."

"What if he is here?" Joanne said. "What do you want with him?"

"I'm his friend," Sweikert said in a rising voice. "The other night he wasn't much help to Alvertone. I thought I'd like to have a little talk with him about it."

"Get out of here," Joanne said, and brought her hand above the counter, the small gun cocked.

Sweikert's good nature vanished like a puff of smoke. "Honey, you better be careful with that. You're playing by a man's rules now."

"Get out of here," she repeated, and came from behind the counter. Sweikert made a quarter turn to face her and she stepped toward him, the gun thrust away from her body. "I mean it. Get out now!"

"Sure," he said softly, watching the gun. Taking a backward step, he edged toward the front door. "Would you really shoot me? A nice girl like you ain't got no business pointin' a gun at a man when he means no harm."

"Just keep backing up," she said, advancing as he retreated.

"Mr. Alvertone ain't goin' to like this," Sweikert said. "No, ma'am, he sure ain't. He's been riled for the past couple days and this is sure goin' to make him worse."

"Take your mouth outside," Joanne urged, and relaxed a little when Sweikert put one hand behind him, groping for the door handle.

Opening it, he stepped half out, then paused. "What about my slicker now? You want a man to get soaked?"

"Get out," she said, and he shrugged, turning away from her.

When she reached for the knob to push the door closed, Sweikert whirled and threw his weight against the panel, pinning Joanne between the frame and the door. She let out a sudden shriek of pain and he clamped a hand over the gun, sweeping it away from her and sending it in a spin into the street.

Taking his weight from the door, he freed her and sent her reeling back inside with a flat handed shove. Then he closed the door behind him. Joanne stood in a crouch, holding her ribs where the door had pinched her. Sweikert said, "I told you you was playin' a man's game."

Taking her by the wrist, he jerked her forward and to her knees. "Where's that sonofabitch Reilly?"

"Behind a door," she gasped. "Go after him, gunman. He'll kill you before you get set."

"Which door?" Sweikert purred. "Tell me, honey, or I'll cave in your skull."

"You won't do that," she said with surprising calm. "Time is running out for you, Sweikert. Someone might come in any time and you'll be dead."

"Then you know I won't fool around with you," he snapped. "Damn it, I want to—" He stopped suddenly, flipping his eyes to the head of the stairs. Lottie Meechum stood there, her mouth open, staring at him.

Joanne screamed, "Run, Lottie!" and Sweikert cuffed her flat with the back of his hand.

The girl whirled and darted from sight. Sweikert cursed and ran toward the stairs. His boots pounded after her. Farther down the hall a door banged shut.

Getting up from the floor, Joanne shook her head to

still the sharp ringing in her ears. A burst of cold air hit her as the front door opened and closed.

Fred Meechum's booming voice filled the room while upstairs a man's shoulder smashed against a door panel, splintering it.

Meechum shook Joanne. "Where's my girl?"

"Hurry," Joanne said, glancing at the shotgun Meechum cradled in his arm. "Sweikert's going to kill Reilly!"

Meechum took the stairs with long strides as Lottie's scream filled the hotel with a long, drawn out wail. At the head of the stairs, Meechum ran forward noiselessly on the balls of his feet. He had no trouble guessing which room they were in for the door hung askew on one hinge and Sweikert's deep voice rang clear as he taunted Reilly. Lottie's frightened pleas were drowned by Sweikert's booming laugh.

Reaching the doorway, Meechum paused the barest fraction of a second to reach a decision; but he had no real trouble making up his mind.

Reilly was sitting up in bed, his face swathed in bandages, his head turned to the sound of Sweikert's voice. Lottie crouched by Reilly, her arms around him and tears staining her cheeks.

Three feet inside the door, Sweikert stood spraddle-legged, his gun cocked and pointed at Reilly.

Meechum said, "Here it is, you sonovabitch," and fired both barrels as Sweikert spun around.

The double load of buckshot whisked the man completely off his feet, carrying him across the room and into the pine dresser which splintered under the impact. Bouncing a little, Sweikert fell in a limp heap to the floor, his gun still cocked and unfired.

"Who is it?" Reilly asked. "That you, Mister Meechum? Speak up, will you?"

For a moment there was no sound in the room save the muted slash of the rain and Lottie's weeping. Finally Meechum cleared his throat. "It's all right, son. Everything's all right now."

"Pa," Lottie said. She moved off the bed toward him, but he held up one hand, stopping her halfway.

"Later," he said huskily. "We all got a lot of time now." Turning out of the room, he walked down the hall, his empty shotgun cradled in his arm, while behind him the smell of black powder hung thick and stinging in the air and a dead man lay on the floor.

He met Owen Frank charging up the stairs. Frank stopped stock still when he saw Meechum's face. Frank didn't ask any questions; he didn't have to.

Breaking the shotgun, Meechum took out the empty brass and put them in his pocket. He reloaded the piece, snapped it closed and said quietly, "I always wanted to shoot one of his kind." Brushing past Owen Frank, he descended the stairs slowly. A moment later the front door opened and closed.

Frank found Joanne in the downstairs back room, bathing her face with a wet towel. An angry mark showed on her cheek where Sweikert had struck her, but aside from that she was unharmed.

"I'll send two of Alvertone's men over to cart him out," he said. "You sure you're all right?"

"Yes. Yes, I'm fine." She passed one hand over her eyes as though wiping away a horrible sight. She shook her head sadly and said, "There's no stopping a war now, is there?"

"No," he admitted.

"All because Reilly loved her," she said. "Because of it a man is dead. Alvertone sent him over to get Reilly, Owen. Can't Will Savage do something with that?"

"Do what?" he asked gently, and put his arm around her. "Did anyone hear Alvertone order Sweikert to kill him?" He patted her shoulder. "Better go to bed and try to get some sleep."

He went to the door and turned. "Don't worry," he said, then crossed the lobby to go out. His coat was rain-soaked by the time he made the shelter of the saloon awning.

Inside, he saw little change. Teepee riders still faced the bar, their hands in plain sight. The farmers waited by the wall, faces impassive, shotguns ready. Alvertone kept gnawing on a cold cigar and Will Savage's face showed a worried frown.

Felix laid down his shotgun as Owen Frank entered, toeing the door shut behind him. Approaching Alvertone, Frank said, "Tough luck, you old pirate. Your pet coon didn't make it."

Alvertone's jaws stopped vising the shredded tobacco. "That's twice you come in this saloon to tell me that."

"The third time I'll just shoot you and do everybody a big favor," Frank said.

"That's enough!" Savage snapped.

"Shut up, Will."

"Dammit, I—"

"Better shut up," Felix murmured, and Savage swung away, tipping up the whisky bottle.

Glancing at Alvertone's men, Frank singled out two with his eyes. "Go over to the hotel," he said, "and haul Sweikert out of there. See that you don't track up the hall either."

Because they were Teepee, they waited. Alvertone said, "Go on. You heard what he said."

No one spoke until the two men walked out. Frank shifted until he leaned against the bar facing Alvertone.

"Tomorrow's election day," he said. "We're going to have a nice, peaceful time of it, aren't we, old man?"

"Wait until tomorrow and find out," Alvertone said. "You'll find out who ramrods this country, Frank. And when my man gets in, you'll be bullet bait for every Teepee gun."

"Sweikert's dead," Frank pointed out. "You got another boy lined up?"

Alvertone laughed and Will Savage's face tightened perceptibly. Even Felix looked startled, for the old man seemed in no position to laugh at anything. Slapping the bar, Burk Alvertone said, "Set 'em up, Felix. We'll drink to the new sheriff—my foreman, Miles Rankin!"

"I told you earlier that you wouldn't get served here," Felix said, dropping his hands below the edge of the bar.

For a minute it was touch and go, and Owen Frank tensed himself for the outcome. Burk Alvertone just smiled and turned away from the bar. "All right, Felix. No more drinks. After the election tomorrow, I'll have some of the boys come around and pull this damned place down around your ears."

"A big chore," the saloon keeper said.

"Teepee likes 'em big," Alvertone said. He nodded to his men. They trooped to the door and went out, leaving the door wide open behind them. Frank walked over and swung it shut, and Will Savage expelled a relieved sigh.

"You still think Alvertone's going to come up on the rope if you win tomorrow?" Frank's voice was faintly amused.

"He's got the bark on tonight," Savage admitted. "Tomorrow, he'll go along with the law, however it comes out."

"We'd better win tomorrow, or there won't be any law." Felix took a healthy drink from his own bottle. He coughed and added, "A man ought to not swill that stuff. It'll kill you."

The farmers filtered out. The wall clock said twelve-fifteen. Frank laid a fifty cent piece on the bar, then crossed the drenched street to the hotel.

CHAPTER 10

Several times during the night Owen Frank awoke and rolled himself a cigarette. Although he was tired, sound sleep eluded him and he dozed fitfully, a shallow rest that left him wakeful, dissatisfied and still weary. A final glance at his pocket watch in the light of a match showed the time to be near six o'clock.

The rain had stopped and he lay for a time listening to the abating drip of water from the eaves. Through the window he saw the first gray light and knew that the day would dawn cold and misty. The sky lightened to a translucent pearl and there seemed no demarcation between it and the land. The wind had retired with the receding rain and the morning held an expectant hush.

The springs protested his movement as he left the bed. Lighting the lamp and stove, he poured water for his shave, smoking another cigarette while it heated.

After stropping his razor to a fine edge, he lathered his face and shaved carefully, paring his sideburns to a scimitar sharpness. He trimmed his mustache neatly, then dried his face and finished dressing.

From his saddlebag he took a clean white shirt and snapped it a few times to remove the wrinkles. Donning this, Frank knotted his string tie, put on his gun and coat and stepped into the hall.

At Joanne Avery's door he rapped softly and listened for an answering movement. The door opened and he entered, sweeping off his hat. A casual glance told him that she had slept but little, for the bed had not been turned back and her light blue robe was sleep-rumpled. A singing fire made the belly of the stove red and a coffee pot gurgled on its top.

Without speaking, she took two cups from a small china cupboard and poured, adding canned milk and sugar. Her loose hair lay bright on her shoulders and her cheeks shone with a freshly scrubbed glow. Her eyes were clear and showed no trace of tears, nor had he expected any. She was the kind of woman who cried little, controlling her emotions.

Taking her cup to the dressing table, Joanne brushed her hair and began to braid it, sipping intermittently at her coffee. Meeting his eyes in the mirror, she said, "Today marks the beginning or the end of a lot of things, doesn't it?"

He shook his head. "The beginning happened a long time ago. The end won't come until men agree that it is the end." He drained his cup and set it on a small table. "You take two kids fighting in the street. One has a black eye and a bloody nose, while the other's got a split lip. Some fellow comes along and pulls them apart and tells them to quit fighting. If they both agree, it ends there. If they don't, they'll take it up again in the alley. When Alvertone's through he's got to know it and admit it. The same goes for the farmers. They'll have to learn to pass a Teepee man on the street without remembering the Hyslips."

She turned on the low stool and faced him, her arms raised to fasten her braids in a coil around her head. "You cut to the heart of everything, don't you? How can you stop the people from thinking about who has been hurt, Owen?"

"Probably can't," he said. "The ones who can't forget will have to go."

"I see," she murmured, and went behind a folding screen. There was the soft rustle of cloth as she dressed. "You don't trust Burk Alvertone at all, do you?"

"No," he said. She emerged from behind the screen in a black dress and presented her back and a row of buttons to be fastened. "Breathe out," he ordered, and began to hook them. "I had four sisters—did I ever tell you?" He grinned when she peeked over her shoulder at him. "Alice, Patricia, Jane and Odessa. Now they're raising Texans of their own."

"Any brothers?"

"Both dead," he said. "Jim was the oldest. He had a run-in with Bat Masterson in Dodge City and didn't come out of it. Jake was killed last year when we fought the homesteaders." He gave her back a small slap. "You're done."

She turned to face him. "You don't like what land wars do to a country, do you?"

"No. They leave only the good tough ones and the bad tough ones. You have to have the in-between too." He touched her arm lightly. "I'll take you to the restaurant for breakfast. Hy Linnet thinks an early service, before the voting starts, would be best."

"All right," she said, and went to the closet for a heavy shawl.

He closed the draught and damper on the stove and snuffed out the lamp. The day's full gray light filtered into the room and they went out and down the stairs.

The sleepy clerk nodded briefly to them as they passed by. Pausing on the hotel porch, Owen Frank glanced up and down the street. Between the sidewalks stretched a churned morass of mud and the boards were slippery from tracks left by men crossing from side to side.

The buildings looked dreary and watersoaked and a heavy mist lay sodden over the land. Frank was surprised at the thick flow of traffic. Farm wagons cluttered the street, patient women sitting on the high seats, their children-chattering in the back.

Of Alvertone or the Teepee hands there was no sign, but their ponies were in evidence hitched here and there along the street. Across from them, Felix had locked his saloon and pulled the blinds. The town seemed curiously dead in spite of the farmers who cruised the boardwalks on both sides.

Leaving the porch, Frank and Joanne walked to the restaurant and chose a corner table. Frank pulled out a chair for her and took his place on the other side, putting his hat on the floor. They gave their order, taking their coffee while they waited.

Joanne Avery sat quiet for a time, her fingers laced together. Only in her eyes was there a clue to the sadness she tried to mask. "I just can't think of him as dead," she said.

"What is death?" he asked. "If he had simply moved away to a far place where you couldn't see him, you wouldn't feel this way. You'd be remembering him pleasantly. Well, he has moved away, Joanne. There's really no difference. Why can't you think of it that way?"

When she raised her eyes to his he saw through the veil that usually obscured her inner self and an answering interest welled up in him. "Do you always know just the right thing to say?" She smiled and her somber mood passed.

Their breakfast of wheatcakes and sausages arrived and they ate in silence. By the time they were half finished Hy Linnet came in, dressed in a stiff suit. He paused by the table and doffed his hat. "Will a half hour be all right, Miss Avery?"

"That will be fine, Hy," she said. Going out, Linnet passed Will Savage coming in. The sheriff saw Frank and the girl and approached, puffing his cheeks against the sharp chill in the air.

Pulling a chair around without invitation, Savage sat down. "I'll have a buggy come around for you, Joanne."

"Thank you, Will, but I'd rather walk." She saw that her contrariness flustered him as it always did, and she could not help but compare him with Owen Frank. In some ways they were so much alike and yet at the same time not alike at all.

In Savage there was that solid stubbornness that made no allowance for another's opinions. There was little bend to him, and even when he did give in, he did so without grace. She was convinced that if it had not been for the approaching funeral, Will Savage would have argued with her about the buggy, ending up in open anger at her refusal. Each man was singular in intent, driving his will against that of other men's, but beneath Owen Frank's determination lay a broad understanding. This was lacking in Will Savage.

"It's beginning to mist outside," Savage said. "That's a half-mile walk to the cemetery."

"I won't melt, Will. But thank you for your consideration."

Savage's face showed a fleeting frustration and he snapped the end from a cigar with his teeth, raking a match with undisguised annoyance. To Owen Frank, he said, "We're polling at the Wells Fargo office. Linnet, Blankenship and Felix are going to stand over the ballot box to see it isn't stuffed."

"You think Alvertone would be that stupid?"

"I guess not," Savage agreed, and laughed. "I'm not a damn bit worried. I'll get the vote of the decent people and that'll put me in for another four years."

"Tell me the difference," Frank asked quietly. "Where's the line, Will?"

"Agh," Savage said, and scraped back his chair. "That's your trouble, Owen—you can't believe in men." The sheriff tipped his hat to Joanne and stalked out.

"Are you ready?" Frank asked.

"In a minute," she said. Then she faltered. "Owen, I'm afraid I'll cry and I don't want to."

"I've heard it said that's the story of a woman's life—crying."

"Not my life," she said.

"No, not yours," he agreed. "Your life would have to be full. Not very sedate, I'm afraid. There's too much living in you, Joanne—too much love to waste energy on tears. You remind me of the solitary eye of a fire in the middle of a long night, where the wind is blowing cool out of the west and the land is flat and unbroken for miles around. A man travels a path for a long time, making pictures in his mind and he'll cover a lot of ground, trying to find the things that fit those pictures. But they're like gold, often hunted and rarely found, so a man tells himself the fun is in the hunting. Only it isn't so. When I came to Painted Rock all I had was pictures, but I don't need them any more. Not now I don't."

Placing her hands flat on the table, she watched him with a breathless unbelief. "Owen—" she began, but then the door opened and Fred Meechum came in.

The big man saw Frank immediately and came over,

setting his heavy boots down hard with each step. He nodded to Joanne but his business was with Frank.

"I'm taking the boy to my camp," he said, and his tone defied Frank to object.

"You sure Reilly won't cast a shadow of shame on the name of Meechum?"

Color mounted Meechum's heavy cheeks, but he let it pass. "I had that one coming, I guess. I want him, Frank. I made a bad mistake."

"That's what a man does best," Frank agreed. "You talked to Reilly about this?"

"Yeah," Meechum said. "I wouldn't blame him if he hated me."

"Reilly's not that kind," Owen said, glancing at Meechum's shotgun. "Don't vote until after Teepee votes," he reminded the big man. "Tell that to your friends."

"I'll tell 'em," Meechum said, and went out.

Finishing his coffee, Owen Frank studied Joanne over the rim of the cup. Their eyes clung together for a long moment. Before Meechum came in there had been something vital between them and Frank wanted to bring it back. He could read the same desire clearly in her eyes, but the magic spell had been broken and he could not conjure it up again.

He checked his watch and said, "We can't put it off any longer, Joanne. Linnet will be waiting for you."

"All right," she said, and stood up, waiting while he paid for the meal. Taking her arm, he opened the door and they stepped out into the dismal daylight. A few shops were open on the cheerless street, but for the most part the town had closed down in respect for Gus Avery.

Owen Frank and Joanne walked to the cross street and turned toward the knoll south of town.

The cemetery nestled in a small grove of jackpine and Linnet's wagon was already there, the caskets on the ground covered with a wide canvas.

A misty rain began to seep from the sky and Joanne pulled the shawl over her head, clutching it under her chin. The fine drops silvered the hair framing her face.

Behind them, the homesteaders mounted their wagons and followed up the hill at a slow walk. By the time they had gone halfway to the top, the entire population of the grove was strung out behind them.

As they neared the cemetery, Frank saw Doctor Harbison's spring wagon to one side, and three men finishing the newly dug graves. The fourth casket, tawny pine like the others, sat a rod away, for this contained Sweikert and had been brought in a separate wagon.

When the wagons were parked, the farmers got down and gave a hand to their women. Linnet waited, bareheaded, a Bible in his hands, and after they gathered in a shivering knot he began his sermon.

Not being wordy by nature, he talked only of the good in man's heart, discounting the hardship and heartbreak that made up man's life. Throughout the sermon, Frank watched the play of emotions on Joanne's face.

She was thinking of her father and the legacy he had left her. Far more valuable than the hotel was the intangible richness of spirit he had nurtured within her through their years together. He had tried to teach her the shaded values in living and when she looked at Owen Frank she realized what they were, for here stood the kind of man her father had urged her to seek, cautioning her against accepting anything less.

As a child she had been unhappy moving from place to place. The process of adjustment to new scenes and faces had frightened her, and as she grew older she became convinced that she hated the pilgrim life. Now this same wanderlust in Owen Frank alarmed her. Yet, as she recalled that early life with her father, a part of her mind refuted the sadness and a flood of warm memory rushed in to fill the vacuum left by her first grief. For a few isolated moments she stood in the drizzling rain and remembered only the pleasant things, the happiness and laughter she had shared with her father.

The rain thickened. Several of the farmers glanced at the sky. Concluding his sermon, Linnet nodded to the three men and they lowered the caskets, one by one. A moment later the first spadeful of dirt thudded on the pine boards and a woman began to weep.

Frank turned Joanne away and they walked slowly down the hill toward Painted Rock. She did not speak for some time.

"There was no family to cry for them," she said at last. "The Hyslips, I mean." She tightened her grip on his arm. "He was a lot like you, Owen—my father. All his life he had the itch to see new things. When I was small, we lived in one gold camp after another. Later it was something else to make him move. He saw the elephant a hundred times and danced with all the wheeligo girls. Laughter, that's what he liked to hear most of all. People being happy."

"He had no regrets," Frank said. "You thought he did, but he didn't. That's what he left you, Joanne—the sound of laughter. What else can a man leave behind him that's more valuable?"

She thought, *how like my father. That's what he would have said*. At that moment the old doubts returned and she wondered if she could be satisfied with just that much from life. She could not find the answer and it troubled her.

Behind them, the farmers' wagons began to move off the hill, pestered by the increasing rain. The men at the cemetery still bent over their tasks, piling the dirt into place.

When they reached the corner of Buffalo and Riot, Joanne halted and looked back. The men were small figures, blurred by rain and distance. Suddenly two tears spilled over her lower lids and slid down her cheeks.

"It's hard to say good-bye," she whispered. "I didn't think it would be so hard."

They walked to the hotel. Once inside, she dried her eyes and said, "I'll be all right now, Owen."

"I'll bet that Gus knew you'd be all right," he said. Her lips changed subtly, becoming full and inviting. He bent toward her and she responded to his kiss softly, touching him only with her lips.

Understanding his impatience to be on the street, she said, "Take care, Owen."

"A lifetime habit," he assured her, and went out the door, his coat pulled tight around his neck to seal out the rain. Across the street, Felix emerged from his saloon and paused to lock the door behind him. Spotting Owen Frank, he crossed the muddy street, lifting his feet high with each step like a dainty cat. He stomped heavily on the boardwalk, leaving broad splashes of mud around him.

"We're going to open the polls in ten minutes. That suit you?"

"Run it to please yourself," Frank said, and glanced up

and down Buffalo Street. "Where's Alvertone and his crew?"

"In the mercantile," Felix said worriedly. "They've been all over town, putting the pinch on the merchants. It's a toss-up which way it's going to go. The farmers are scared, Owen. You can see it in their faces."

"Sure they're scared," Frank said. "Where's Savage?"

"In his office. You going to help him?" Felix pursed his heavy lips at Frank's nod. "Why are you doing it? There's nothing in it for you."

"Does a man have to get something back for everything he does?"

"Nothing is for nothing," Felix said wisely. "You and I both know that. You came into Painted Rock like a wolf on the howl, but you've changed some since then." He paused for a moment to study the street. "You takin' Joanne Avery with you when you leave?"

"Now you're getting nosy," Frank said, with just enough of a smile to take the sting out of it.

"A failing of mine," Felix admitted. He saw Hy Linnet and Blankenship round the far corner. "See you later, Owen." He hurried off, his mind swinging like a weather-vane in a new direction. The three men clustered together on the boardwalk, talking, then went into the express office.

Frank walked slowly toward the jail on the corner. He entered without knocking. Savage was sitting behind his desk, cleaning a double-barreled shotgun. Savage assembled it and put it aside, folding his hands in a leisurely fashion.

"Need a little help?" Frank asked.

"I'll handle it," Savage said. He lit a cigar and propped his elbows on the desk, puffing until his face blurred through the smoke. "Owen, you just can't get it out of your mind that Burk Alvertone is a real badman, can you?"

"That's right," Frank said, and fashioned a cigarette from a damp sack of makings. "I was in his shoes once and I know how desperate a man can get. I also understand how far he has to go if he wants to come out on top. All the way, Will, all the way." A bit of tobacco spilled from the end of the cyclinder as he licked it into shape. "It's a funny thing—watching a man travel the same road you took once before. But it's bad when you want to tell him that it's no good and know at the same time that you can yell and yell and he'll never hear you."

Leaning back in his chair, Savage laced his hands behind his head and studied Owen Frank, the cigar jutting from between his teeth at a jaunty angle. "For a long time you puzzled me," the sheriff said. "But not any more."

"I'm glad someone has the answers," Frank said.

Savage laughed. "You're running, friend, even when you're standing still. You can't stop running. That's what a conscience will do to you."

"How does yours feel?"

For a moment, Frank thought Savage was going to give him a fight but the sheriff relaxed finally and puffed his cigar. "You think I've coasted along in my job, don't you? Don't bother to tell me—I know what you're thinking. But you're wrong, Owen. Dead wrong. No man can set himself up as judge before the farmers and Alvertone and tell which should go and who should stay. The election has to decide the issue. It will make farmer law or cattleman law, and if the farmers win, Alvertone will stick by the law. That's his way."

"Not this time," Frank said. "He has to win. Can't you see that?"

"He'll lose," Savage said stubbornly. "The day of the thirty thousand acre spread is gone. He'll see it." He threw his cigar into the spittoon. "You know, I ought to hate you, Owen. But I don't and I'll tell you why. There's nothing permanent about you and I know it. Joanne and I —well, you understand how it was between us. If I was a small-minded man, I'd take a gun to you for beating my time, but actually you haven't. When this is over, your feet will itch but she won't go with you. Knowing that, I'm not worried, because a woman forgets in a hurry."

"You've got a practical mind," Frank said, a slight edge to his voice.

"Thanks for the offer to help," Savage said, and closed out the tall Texan by focusing his attention on the loading of his shotgun. Frank let himself out and wandered up Buffalo Street.

At the far corner, Burk Alvertone and his crew came out of the mercantile, crowding the full width of the boardwalk. From the flats there came a steady drumming of hooves, and another group of riders pounded across the bridge and pulled in at the hitchrack. This was the remainder of the Teepee crew and they dismounted, joining the others grouped on the boardwalk.

Alvertone and Miles Rankin stood together and slightly in front of the others. They watched Owen Frank steadily as he paced leisurely toward them. No business with Alvertone dictated this approach; just his pride and the need to make them understand that their numbers did not intimidate him.

Stopping before Alvertone and Rankin, Frank tugged his hat low over his eyes and moisture dribbled from the V-crease. With a careful smile he said, "Care to make an election bet, Burk?"

"I wouldn't want to rob you," Alvertone said, the drooping ends of his mustache lifting a little.

Behind Owen Frank and halfway down the street, Hy Linnet came out, yelled, "Polls are open until five o'clock," and went back inside.

Along both sides of the street the farmers waited, eyeing Alvertone's crew with a certain dread. Burk Alvertone nudged Miles Rankin.

"Like a bunch of lost sheep," he said.

"Don't make any trouble today," Frank offered as advice.

"Careful there," Alvertone said, his humor fading rapidly. "We can take you now and swallow you whole."

"Not without getting clawed, you can't." Frank watched Rankin. The man exhibited an eagerness that teetered on the thin edge of action.

"Let's go and vote," Alvertone said. He stepped past Owen Frank, his men following him. Rankin hung back, and when he moved it was toward the tall Texan, with the open intention of walking him down.

"Try it," Frank invited, and measured the sudden flare of ambition that crowded into Rankin's eyes. For a second it was touch and go, and then Rankin discarded the idea. He moved around Frank but jarred him solidly with his shoulder in passing.

Frank watched Teepee file into the express office, emerging again one by one as each made his mark. He watched for ten minutes, then lost interest and turned into the mercantile. Making his way past the piled boxes and hanging merchandise, he paused at the counter where the storekeeper was busy with a ledger.

"A sack of Durham," Frank said, and laid a nickel on the counter. "Alvertone tell you how to vote yet?"

"Maybe," the man admitted.

Grinning, Frank sat on the counter, one leg dangling over the edge. Stripping a wheat paper from the sack, he rolled a cigarette and lit it. "Better play it smart and vote late in the day."

"Are you telling me what to do?" The clerk bristled, but just for show. He was an uncertain mouse caught between two cats. He needed advice, wanting it desperately but afraid the wrong eyes might see it.

"You're a smart man," Frank said softly. "Been in business a long time, and you can't afford to make a mistake now. You've got a window. Why don't you keep watch and see which way it goes? If Alvertone starts shoving the farmers around and scares 'em off, then you'd better vote his way, because each one he can keep away from the poll is a vote for him. But if the farmers put up a battle, then you'd better get off Burk's bandwagon—because Rankin won't beat Savage."

"I see what you mean," the man said. He stroked his chin, the scrape of his whiskers loud in the silence. "You think the farmers will carry the vote?"

Frank shook his head. "The town vote will be the deciding one. Look at it this way. If the town goes for Rankin and the farmers decide to fight, a lot of people are going to get hurt. The farmers might just win, and if they do you're out of business. You think they'd trade with you when you voted against them?"

"Savage has never gone all out for the farmers," the man said doubtfully.

"But he's never gone against them either," Frank said. "If Rankin gets it, look out, because it'll be all for Burk Alvertone then and to hell with everybody else."

"I don't like being in the position to have to decide a thing like this," the merchant said.

"Sink or swim," Frank told him, and went back out to the street. He spent the next hour dropping in one store after another. He made his points, sounded out the merchants and left. Being smart enough to know where a man's loyalty lay, he merely painted a picture of a town that was solid Alvertone.

None of them liked the idea but they saw a way out of it by delaying their votes to the very last. It gave them a fence to straddle, and that was all they asked, for they had to swing to the side that would keep them in business.

Around ten the rain slacked off and Alvertone's men cruised the streets. Their votes had been cast and there was nothing left for them to do but watch and wait. Rankin stayed near the Wells Fargo office, a big man with a gun and a definite surliness stamped in the set of his features.

A dozen farmers clustered together across from the express office, speculating on whether or not the time was ripe. As Frank approached he saw suddenly what Rankin was doing. When another Teepee hand crossed over to take a position beside Rankin, thereby presenting a solid front to the farmers, Owen Frank hurried—for the farmers had started across the street in a purposeful knot and trouble was only a few minutes away.

CHAPTER 11

With a vague uneasiness plaguing him, Will Savage tucked the shotgun beneath his arm and left his office, rounding the corner in time to see Miles Rankin and the Teepee rider take positions flanking the Wells Fargo doorway.

As he grasped the significance of this move, his eyes flicked to the farmers crossing the muddy street. He began to hurry. Although Rankin and his hand were outnumbered three to one, there was no give in them, no fear of the farmers.

The homesteaders paused on the boardwalk's edge, uncertain. Then a tall man named Harris shrugged and moved toward the express office door. Owen Frank halted beside this drama and waited with a fine-drawn patience.

As Harris bracketed the doorway, Rankin reached

out and fastened a hand in the man's coat sleeve. "You don't want to go in there, mister."

Harris tried to jerk free of Rankin's grip, but Rankin held on doggedly. The Teepee ramrod smiled, and something in his eyes kept Harris's friends from interfering.

Coming along the walk, Will Savage pushed a farmer aside to break this up, but the Teepee rider stepped in front of him. "No trouble here," the man said, and Savage frowned.

"Release that man, Rankin," Savage said, and swung his head to one side for a clear view. The cowboy moved with him, blocking him again. "Get out of my way," Savage told him.

"You're getting your nose out of joint," the man said. "Rankin and him's havin' a little talk, that's all."

"You want to go to jail, Rusty?"

The rider laughed. "Be careful, Mister Sheriff. Teepee's in town today and we're not foolin' around."

With Rankin's grip still tight on Harris' sleeve, the farmer stood docilely, wanting to answer this threat but lacking the sand for it.

"How you going to vote, pilgrim?" Rankin asked, locking eyes with the farmer. "Vote yourself clean out of the country?" He laughed tauntingly. "I'm going to be the new sheriff. Don't you think you ought to show a little respect to such an important man?" He shook Harris's arm. "Don't you now?"

Frank placed his hand on the farmer's shoulder. Rankin's attention left Harris when he found Frank at his elbow. His eyes narrowed, bracing Frank while he still held Harris.

"Go on in and vote," Frank told Harris, but he looked only at Rankin.

For a moment, the two men's wills seesawed back and forth with the farmer in the middle. Rankin's grip tightened on the farmer's sleeve, and beyond them, Will Savage stood spraddle legged, still blocked off by the Teepee rider.

"Go on in," Frank repeated.

Harris tried to move away but was held by Rankin's strength.

"All right," Frank said. "You stand there and hold him, Rankin. The rest of you—go in there and vote."

There was a murmur and then they moved around these three men, entering the express office. Rankin's eyes filled with a sudden flare of temper.

"Now, turn him loose," Frank ordered, and knocked the Teepee foreman's hand away with a chopping blow.

The cloth gave way and Harris's sleeve sported a long rent, but he lifted his shoulders and went inside before Rankin could grab him again. The Teepee foreman regarded Frank with slitted eyes, but he made no attempt to push a fight.

"Now get the hell out of here," Frank said, and Rankin swayed as though in a heavy wind. Frank understood this, for he felt the same force. Here was the old challenge, an acid eating on a man's pride.

"The day ain't over yet," Rankin said. He spun on his heel, gave the Teepee rider a curt nod and plunged across the street to the opposite boardwalk. The sheriff and Frank waited for a moment, then walked down the street together.

"That's the first," Frank said. "This is going to be a long day."

"I never thought Teepee would dare to try and stop the polls," Savage said. He had caught a glimmer of the truth and was still reluctant to believe it. He stopped and shifted his shotgun. "I'm going to talk to Burk. If he'll keep his men off the streets it might prevent trouble."

"He'll tell you to get the farmers off the streets. He'll tell you he paid for the planks in the boardwalks and they're his by prior rights."

"You don't believe in anything, do you?" Savage exhibited the bared edge of his temper before leaving the boardwalk and stomping across the muddy street.

Rain still filtered down in a thick drizzle and Owen Frank sought the shelter of a building overhang, content to stand there and watch the movement of men up and down the street. Harris and his friends dribbled from the Wells Fargo office and several more farmers went inside. Teepee hands were sprinkled along the other side, mingling with the farmers. Now and then one would ram a farmer with a shoulder or elbow. Twice they crowded a man off the boardwalk into the mud of the street, but the farmers in each case let it pass, staring at the ground until the threat had passed.

At the end of an hour, the movement had come to a near standstill and the Teepee men were neatly deployed. Each man had picked a farmer and hovered near, not saying anything or touching him, but holding him there with a silent menace.

The voting had stopped.

Will Savage emerged from the feed store, angling across the street toward Owen Frank. The sheriff removed his hat and slapped it impatiently against his leg to remove the water. There was a stubborn anger on his handsome face.

He said, "Go ahead, Frank. Say I told you so."

"I did tell you, didn't I?" Frank tried to hide his smile but it broke past the tranquillity of his lips and crept into his eyes.

Across the street, a big farmer had tired of waiting and stepped to the edge of the boardwalk, followed immediately by a Teepee rider. As the farmer stepped into the street, the rider rammed him in the back, driving the farmer face down in the mire.

A ripple of laughter floated down Buffalo Street and the farmers exchanged glances, understanding fully what was happening. The man in the mud pushed himself to his hands and knees and turned a blackened face to the Teepee hand.

"Cowboy," he said, "you just bought yourself some fun."

Savage made a move to leave the sheltering overhang, but Frank halted him with a pull on his coat. "Let 'em alone," Frank said. "This may break it up."

The farmer came to his feet with a swoop, diving toward the cowboy, head down like a charging bull. Stepping nimbly to one side, the Teepee rider whipped up a knotted fist and arched the farmer over backward into the mud again. Then he jumped, both feet extended.

With a twist, the farmer avoided the murderous boots. He wrapped his huge arms around the cowboy's legs, bringing him down like a tall tree. Mud shot up in a dark shower as the rider hit, and then the two men were locked together, rolling and thrashing.

The farmer fought free and backed away to gain his feet. When the rider tried to rise, the farmer snapped a fist in

"You did a good job here and the reason ain't worth a hill of beans, not even to yourself. You don't want to leave here. You want to keep this badge because it gives you a reason for stayin' and saves your pride.

"Dammit, shut up!" Frank slapped the bar with the flat of his hand. Felix glanced toward the door and a change came over his face, drawing Frank's attention around.

He saw Joanne Avery standing in the doorway. She wore a pair of men's blue jeans, a blue flannel shirt, and a light Mackinaw. Behind her, he could see a blanket roll and a canvas valise.

"I got tired of waiting for you," she said tremulously, and moved along the bar until she nearly touched him. A small smile lifted the ends of her lips and there was no reservation in her eyes. "No matter what, I found I had to have you, Owen—on any terms."

Understanding how strong her pride was, and how dear her dreams, he knew what this cost her and it chipped away the last stone between them. For the first time in his life he knew real humility and recognized the uselessness of his life as it had been. He had never bargained with any man, not even himself, answering only the dictates of his own will. Now he saw how wrong he had been, and he felt a new sense of ease run through him as he acknowledged this bargain with himself.

Taking her arm, he smiled and watched her return it. Even now, she still meant to put her own hopes aside for him because of her love. At the door, Frank glanced back and found Felix watching him, his eyes haunted with worry.

Frank said, "Can you find someone to turn my horse into the corral? Just throw my gear in the loft."

Like a smear wiped from glass, the worry disappeared from the saloon keeper's eyes and he smiled. Joanne turned Frank so the lamplight fell on his face and her voice was vibrant with hope. "This is for good, Owen? You're sure? I couldn't stand it if you were ever sorry."

"This is for good," he told her, and cupped her face in his hands. His kiss was gentle and alive and there was no past to trouble him now. There was only tomorrow, and a life that would be full and satisfying.

THE END

159

Will Cook is the author of numerous outstanding Western novels as well as historical frontier fiction. He was born in Richmond, Indiana, but was raised by an aunt and uncle in Cambridge, Illinois. He joined the U.S. cavalry at the age of sixteen but was disillusioned because horses were being eliminated through mechanization. He transferred to the U.S. Army Air Force in which he served in the South Pacific during the Second World War. Cook turned to writing in 1951 and contributed a number of outstanding short stories to *Dime Western* and other pulp magazines as well as fiction for major smooth-paper magazines such as *The Saturday Evening Post*. It was in the *Post* that his best-known novel *Comanche Captives* was serialized. It was later filmed as *Two Rode Together* (Columbia, 1961) directed by John Ford and starring James Stewart and Richard Widmark. Sometimes in his short stories Cook would introduce characters that would later be featured in novels, such as Charlie Boomhauer who first appeared in *Lawmen Die Sudden* in *Big-Book Western* in 1953 and is later to be found in *Badman's Holiday* (1958) and *The Wind River Kid* (1958). Along with his steady productivity, Cook maintained an enviable quality. His novels range widely in time and place, from the Illinois frontier of 1811 to southwest Texas in 1905, but each is peopled with credible and interesting characters whose interactions form the backbone of the narrative. Most of his novels deal with more or less traditional Western themes—range wars, reformed outlaws, cattle rustling, Indian fighting—but there are also romantic novels such as *Sabrina Kane* (1956) and exercises in historical realism such as *Elizabeth, by Name* (1958). Indeed, his fiction is known for its strong heroines. Another common feature is Cook's compassion for his characters who must be able to survive in a wild and violent land. His protagonists made mistakes, hurt people they care for, and sometimes succumb to ignoble impulses, but this all provides an added dimension to the artistry of his work.